STIFF IN THE SAND

CAPE HOPE MYSTERIES

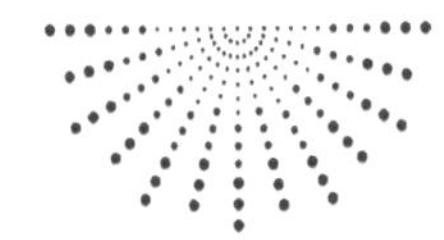

WINNIE REED

STIFF IN THE SAND

CAPE HOPE MYSTERIES BOOK ONE

New jobs can be murder...

At least, that's what it seems like to Emma Harmon of Cape Hope. She's got a new job blogging about food and she's super-thrilled to be traveling to a new resort to sample the fare and meet local celebrities. One of who is First-Kiss-Robbie. The first boy to kiss her, he's a famous chef now.

She finds out her photographer is a hot guy with a major chip on his shoulder. More like an iceberg, considering the way Deke treats her.

She's not so thrilled when she discovers a body in the sand dunes. One with a knife sticking out of him. A chef knife. Robbie's chef knife.

She's even less thrilled when she makes the mistake of handling the knife.

Now, she's under suspicion and Detective McHottie's got his eye on her—and not in a good way.

Can she find the real killer before she becomes his target?

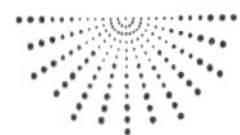

The thing about living in a Quaint-with-a-capital-Q beachfront town was the assumptions people made. Figuring life lived by the beach in a town filled with adorable gingerbread-style Victorian homes must be nothing but fun and sun all year long.

People made plenty of assumptions, most of which were eye-roll-worthy. No, my life was not chock-full of charm and romance, no matter how beautiful the area in which I'd grown up. And it was beautiful, no doubt. In no way did I take for granted the stunning architecture, the history, the colorful characters who could afford to live in some of those stunning homes.

Because let's face it, people with that sort of money could afford to be colorful, too. The rest of us would just be called kooks if we walked around the way they did.

Another assumption, growing up working in my mother's café made me the luckiest kid in the entire world. Because how hard could it be to run a café and chat up the customers, right?

Wrong. Very wrong. Even years later, long after I'd stopped doing anything more than filling in on the occasional day when Mom didn't feel up to working—which was an extremely rare occurrence—I couldn't sleep past five in the morning. Waking up early became a habit deeply ingrained in my psyche, one which tended to irk the living daylights out of my boyfriend.

Or, ex-boyfriend. Speaking of assumptions, I had assumed he would be faithful to me and only me.

Hadn't I learned by then that it was no good to assume things? That just because something looked a certain way didn't make it so? Just because Landon was perfect on the surface—like a three-layer sour cream chocolate cake with whipped ganache frosting, tall and majestic and tempting—didn't mean he wasn't dry and crumbly on the inside.

The one thing a sour cream chocolate cake was not supposed to be.

The one thing a live-in, practically-ready-to-pop the question boyfriend wasn't supposed to be. Unfaithful, that is. Not dry and crumbly.

I was never great with analogies.

And that was unfortunate, seeing as how my new job would require me to come up with a few clever turns of phrase.

"It'll be just like writing your blog," my sister assured me, sitting down with a pair of blueberry muffins at a table by the window looking out over Main Street. "Just, you know. With more words."

I picked at one of the plump blueberries and popped it in my mouth, savoring the sweetness as it burst open. Mom always made a point of using the highest-quality ingredients, and the many blueberry farms within driving distance of town made these particular muffins my favorite of all her baked goods.

I'd mixed them up and baked them enough times to know the process by heart. I might even have been able to pull it off while blindfolded. The trick was tossing the berries in flour before gently stirring them into the batter. This helped them stay uniformly distributed throughout the final product rather than sinking to the bottom of the muffin cups.

"Yeah. More words. You're a genius, Darce." I couldn't help but roll my eyes at my well-meaning but somewhat clueless sister. What would she think if I told her there was nothing to running a bookstore but keeping the books dusted and making sure people paid before leaving?

Darcy eyed me over the rim of her coffee cup, the steam fogging up her glasses. Behind those glasses was a pair of kind, knowing, sky-blue eyes I had always envied. Mine tended to vary between gray and light blue depending on what I wore.

Hence my penchant for blue clothing.

"It's just that I didn't need a blow to my ego right now," I reminded her. Two years older and every ounce the big sister, I had been coming to her with my problems for as long as I had them. Granted, this was a lot weightier than complaining about the boy down the street who stole my favorite Barbie and wouldn't give her back.

I doubted I could send Darcy after Landon to beat him up. No matter how much I wanted to. And it wasn't like she could hand me back my bruised, broken heart, either, which was what he'd stolen. Along with my trust and three years of my life.

"Three years when you could've been working on grandchildren for me." It was like the woman read my mind. Sylvia Harmon—she hadn't changed her name back after the divorce from Dad, since her name was connected with everything café-related—breezed in from the back with a tray of fresh scones. "He took that opportunity away from me, the philanderer."

"Mom." I folded my hands, pleading. "Tell me you don't randomly talk about my personal issues with customers. Please, I beg you." The café wasn't open yet and wouldn't be for another ten minutes, so at least nobody but the three of us had heard that little quip.

"Me?" Her eyes widened, reminding me of an owl. Which was how I knew she had, in fact, told the entire town my personal business the minute I'd called after kicking that no-good jerkface out of what used to be our apartment.

"Wonderful." I sighed. It had been two weeks since I'd returned home after filling in for Darcy at the bookstore which adjoined the café to find my would-be fiancé—I'd been so sure a proposal was coming up, I wanted to smack myself for being that naïve—entertaining a girl from his office. In our bed.

News could spread pretty far in three weeks. Heck, it could spread in a day in a town as close-knit as Cape Hope. Especially when one of the parties involved was the daughter of two of the town's most beloved personalities.

The other personality being my father. Detective George

Harmon, one of the town's finest, somebody who'd devoted his life to keeping everybody safe. I wished one assumption were true, that when a girl had a cop for a father, he would do mean, horrible, terrible things to any fool who decided to cheat on her.

"Maybe taking a job which involves travel isn't the best idea for you right now," Mom mused from behind the counter. "You need to be close to home at a time like this, Emma."

Darcy and I exchanged a glance. She knew how I felt about this.

The fact was, before Landon's roll in the hay with his bimbo coworker, I'd been considering turning down the chance at working for Haute Cuisine, a publisher with magazines and online publications based all over the country. They published pieces about new restaurants, food trends, up-and-coming chefs and hot spots from coast to coast, along with the typical recipes, kitchen product reviews, and other food-related articles.

In other words, I'd been reading their work since I was old enough to grab Mom's discarded magazines from the coffee table and make sense of what the pictures meant.

The job came with travel, which when I thought I was on the verge of getting engaged was a no-no. I couldn't have imagined being without that creep. No wonder he'd urged me to take it. More time without my hanging around, messing up his fun.

Now? The thought of not being out of town and away from him and his new girlfriend turned my stomach. I couldn't stand that kind of humiliation.

But considering the fact that my mom hung around Cape Hope after Dad started dating somebody closer to my age than Mom's... It was best to keep my thoughts to myself.

"The first assignment is practically right up the road," Darcy reminded her, stepping in before I had the chance to embarrass myself or our mother. "Remember? The resort they're opening in Paradise City. The one Robbie's Executive Chef for."

"Of course!" At the mention of Robbie Klein, her beloved former apprentice, Mom's face lit up. "Sweet Robbie. Please, give him my love. I can't wait to take the drive up there someday soon and see how far he's come."

"I'll let him know," I promised, glad my sister's deft engineering had turned the conversation toward more pleasant things. When Marsha, my new editor, had offered me the task of covering the resort opening I'd jumped at the chance. Writing about Robbie's food would be a pleasure, since he'd been wowing me in the kitchen since we were teenagers.

Including the one time we smooched in the walk-in, but nobody needed to know about that besides the two of us. That was a wow-worthy experience.

"I bet your editor loved the personal angle you can bring to the piece," Darcy observed, standing and brushing crumbs from herself and the table before taking her plate and cup to the counter.

"Uh, I didn't tell her about the personal angle," I confessed, twirling a strand of hair around my finger and trying to look innocent. We all shared the same shade of honey-blonde, all the Harmon girls.

"Why not?"

"I was afraid she'd take the job away if she knew. I'm supposed to be objective. And honestly, it's the perfect first assignment to get my feet wet. Not thirty minutes up the road, writing about a friend in an area I'm already familiar with. I didn't want to lose the chance." I blinked. "Do you think I was wrong?"

The thing about having a sister like Darcy was knowing I never had to think very much over the right or wrong of anything. She would tell me, sure enough.

"Not super wrong," she decided. "But marginally."

"Thanks," I muttered before taking a huge bite of muffin. Nothing like sugary carbs when I was unsure of myself.

Darcy hurried next door to finish prepping *First Edition*, the bookstore she'd owned for the last two years, for the morning's customers. Having a bakery/café and bookstore sitting side-by-side made all the sense in the world. Her patrons would often bring their new books into *Sweet Nothings*, and so long as they promised not to spill all over the place, my sister allowed paper coffee cups into the store.

Only once had anybody tripped and sploshed coffee all over a row of books, and they'd been gracious enough to purchase each damaged copy. Somebody out there owned a dozen copies of the same pulpy murder mystery. Lucky them.

"I could use a little help back here this morning," Mom prompted. "You know how it is. Everybody likes to get the last day of the work week moving with a caffeinated treat."

My smile was tight. "Mom. You know I normally would, but I'm sure everybody knows by now. I don't think I can face the whole town or even part of the town this morning."

"What? Nobody knows anything, sweetheart." My mother, sweet lying soul she was, made a sign of the cross over her chest. "If they do, they didn't hear it from me."

I was almost sure nothing could be further from the truth.

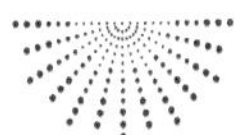

"Emma! Back from the dead, I see." Mr. Hutchins, old ladies' man that he was, dropped me a wink as he slapped his newspaper on the counter hard enough to make me twitch. He had a habit of doing that. I was pretty sure it had to do with failing hearing and not realizing how loud he was.

"Rumors of my death have been greatly exaggerated." I handed over a cup of coffee. Black, strong, nothing fancy or foamy for an old Marine who informed anybody who'd listen that he still walked five miles a day.

He looked me up and down, clicking his tongue in mock dismay. "Don't know what was wrong with that boy's noggin," he muttered mournfully.

I was going to kill my mother.

I pretended not to know what he was talking about, then encouraged the next customer to step forward. If it wasn't for Mr. Hutchins' broad shoulders, I would've seen Mrs. Merriweather's impressive confection of a hat and known she was next.

I had to hand it to her. The lady had style. Her husband had served on the city council for decades before being voted mayor. Gertie Merriweather had been trying to raise money for a statue in his honor ever since his passing a year earlier.

"How's the statue fund going?" I asked, pulling out a sheet of waxed paper so I could fetch her customary blueberry muffin. I could vouch for their goodness.

"Better every day!" She was maybe the most optimistic person I'd ever known, and her hats reflected that optimism. Today's was a doozy: straw, wide-brimmed, wrapped in butter-yellow tulle which hung down in a veil in the back. On the crown was perched a bluebird nestled in silk daffodils and bluebells.

"That's good to hear." I rang her up and handed her the change, which she generously dropped into the tip jar.

"I was so sorry to learn of your unfortunate situation with that Landon fellow," she whispered loud enough to be heard down the street. "I hiss at him whenever I see him on the street."

"Oh, please. You don't have to do that." But she was already chatting with Mom, who was in the process of wiping down one of the pastel-colored tables.

"I told her," Mom said like I wasn't listening, "with this new job of hers and all the travel she'll be doing, there's bound to be a new man in her future."

That was roughly the point where I wanted to die. Maybe I'd find a previously undiscovered hole in the floor and fall in and never come out. "I thought you weren't telling anybody my private business," I called out in a singsong voice when Mom walked past with a dishpan filled with plates and cups.

She only waved a hand. "Oh, Gertie doesn't count. She's practically family."

That was the problem. In a town where Mom's café had been the central point of gossip for a quarter century, everybody was family. At least it seemed more people than not were on Team Emma.

I hadn't even known until that morning that there was a Team Emma.

When the morning rush had calmed to a slow trickle of folks wandering in and out, I removed my apron. "I'd better head home. I have to get ready for tonight. I don't even know what I'm going to wear." Was anything in my closet worthy of the grand opening of a new resort?

Mom eyed me up and down. "Be sure to look your best, no matter what you end up in."

"Gee, thanks. I'll keep that in mind."

"I'm just saying, you never know the sort of men who attend these events…"

"Mom. Please. I just got the bleeding to stop not that long ago. Give my heart a little time to heal now, okay?" I kissed her cheek, taking in a blend of scents I would always associate with her: powdered sugar, coffee, chocolate, vanilla. If anybody ever made a perfume out of that combination I'd buy stock in the company.

She meant well, all of her digging into my personal life. Complaints about grandchildren aside, it hurt her to know I'd been hurt. Maybe because she understood better than most what it meant to hand so much of her life over to somebody and have that investment of time and trust turn out badly.

Through it all, she was a hopeless romantic. I couldn't help but respect her refusal to give up on love.

Main Street was its usual splash of color on an otherwise gray day, the shops and art galleries lining both sides of the thoroughfare showing off their striped awnings and lush potted plants out front. I hoped the weather would hold out for the opening of the resort—from the conceptual art I'd already studied in prep for the night, I knew there was a huge outdoor space which overlooked the beach. It would've been a waste to not have it decorated and ready to be enjoyed on opening night.

But what did I know? This was my first assignment.

Assignment. Like the journalist I was always supposed to be. At least, according to the degree I was still paying off. It sounded so official. I had an assignment.

I had a job, full-stop. Finally, something my parents could agree on; how important it was for me to have a real job. Blogging wasn't a real job to either of them, even if it had provided comfortably enough for me over the years.

My apartment sat over a pizza shop three blocks from Main, and I waved to Mr. Angelo through the window before opening the unobtrusive little door and jogging up to the second floor. Mr. Angelo and his cheesy, delightfully greasy pies had gotten me through my two weeks of post-Landon fallout.

Now, kicking off my shoes upon entering the familiar space, I made it a point to avoid the mess still waiting to be cleaned up. I'd managed to clear away the ice cream containers, pizza crusts, takeout boxes, and empty wine bottles, so at least it looked like an actual human being lived there now.

But he was still everywhere, lingering. In the bedding heaped in one corner, waiting to be taken out to the curb. I had replaced it after flipping the mattress and spraying disinfectant to remove any Bimbo germs.

The minute my checks started coming in, I was buying a new mattress. Maybe an entirely new bed.

One of his neckties had managed to land in the back corner of the closet, unnoticed in the frenzy to get all remnants of him out of my life. Blue with a lighter blue stripe. Big surprise, it was one I'd purchased for him. I picked it up and tossed it into the corner with the bedding.

What mattered right now was finding the right outfit for the evening and making a good impression. I pulled a half-dozen dresses from the closet and spread them over the bed, then called the person I always turned to when I had to pretend to be fancy.

"Woof. What time is it?" Raina was still partially wearing a sleep mask when she answered my FaceTime request.

"Uh… eleven-ish? In the morning? Should I not have called? Are you sick?"

"No, no, no," she mumbled, taking off the mask and rubbing a hand over her face. "I was out until last call with some old friends of the family. Their parents and my parents were friends so we had to be up in each other's lives all the time. It was rough."

"That bad, huh?"

"I didn't even like them very much when we were kids, but I thought I should be nice and accept the invite." She sat up in bed with a groan. "So what's up?"

"For one thing, I am offended by how flawless you look when you're only just rolling out of bed." Not a chocolate-brown strand was out of place, silky and lightly tousled. Not a smudge of mascara under her sea green eyes, either. She could party until all hours and wake up looking like a goddess.

"Shush. I do not."

"Anyway, I needed your advice. Tonight's the night."

"Oh, right! Gosh, I forgot. So what do you need? Outfit ideas?"

"Yup." I flipped the camera around so she could see the bed and its many dresses. "What do you think? Is this an LBD occasion? Or do I go with a bold red? Keep in mind, I'll be wearing a throw or sweater or something. It's still only April." And that sea breeze could be killer at night.

She tapped a finger to her chin. "You don't want to stand out. This isn't your night. You can never go wrong with a little black dress. You have that shawl I gave you for your birthday, right? The one with roses embroidered on it?"

"Ooh, yes! And my gold sandals."

"There you go. Wear those gold hoops I like so much." I went to my jewelry box and found them. She gave me a thumbs up. "There you go. Classy, elegant, but not flashy."

"I would walk around looking like a hobo if it wasn't for you." When she didn't smile. In fact, she looked concerned—I giggled. "It was a joke, Ray."

"What's that in the corner? On the floor?" One of her eyebrows was arched almost clear off her forehead. "Is it what I think it is? Oh, Emma. Come on."

"What?" I forgot she could see the entire bedroom. "The bedding and whatnot?"

"Why haven't you thrown it away?" Her voice was gentle, at least. "Honey, you shouldn't keep that around. If only for hygienic reasons."

"I sprayed it with enough disinfectant to almost choke myself." Like that mattered. I sank to the bed with a sigh. "I'm not having an easy time with this. I'm getting better. And I'm gonna bag that stuff up and put it out today. I promise."

"Don't make me drive down there and see for myself."

"What if I want you to drive down?" When she didn't smile, I sighed again. "Okay, Mom. I'll do it. And thanks for the advice. Get your day started. I'll let you know how it goes tonight."

"Tell First Kiss Robbie I said hi!" she teased before ending the call. I made a mental note to stop thinking of him as First Kiss Robbie before I made a fool out of myself during his big opening.

CHAPTER THREE

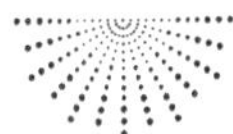

It seemed a little silly, handing my bubblegum pink Bug over to a valet so it could be parked in the brand-spanking-new garage behind the resort. Mine was hardly the sort of car a kid in a rented tuxedo parked for someone, but it was opening night and all the stops were being pulled out.

I adjusted my fringed shawl—probably the nicest thing I owned, thanks to Raina—and looked around, absorbing the details. Everything was so new. So shiny. Floodlights illuminated the entirely glass façade of the fifteen-story hotel, swinging back and forth. I blinked against the glare. It would be even more striking once the sun set in an hour or so.

A neon sign at the very top of the tower proclaimed the resort's name far and wide: The Riviera. Palm trees completely out of place in New Jersey lined the long drive leading up to the entrance, and in between them were floodlights pointed up toward the sky. Like James Flynn, the hotel's owner and Robbie—Robert—Klein's business partner, wanted the entire world to flock to his hotel.

I couldn't imagine why they wouldn't. Walking along the path which wound around the resort led me to a gorgeous pool surrounded by cabanas, the beach leading straight up to it. Already people were mingling out there, waitstaff carrying champagne on silver trays.

It was a fantasy world, which was obviously what Flynn had in mind when he'd built it.

But I was there for the food, which led me through plate-glass doors into the restaurant.

So clean, so perfect. Nobody had ever sat here. I ran my hand over the back of a chair—leather, brand-new—and admired the blue, white and silver motif. It was all so fresh, bright, sleek.

"Excuse me." I barely had time to turn around or even acknowledge the man who'd spoken before he pushed his way past.

"No. Excuse me," I muttered, straightening the chair he'd shoved me against.

He didn't seem to notice, too interested in his camera and the shot he was trying to take. "You're in the way," he said as he composed his next shot. "Could you step back and to the left, please?"

I did it, but only because he startled me too badly to argue or ask where he got off being so rude. Besides, something told me he wouldn't pay attention if I spoke.

Once he'd snapped a few pics, he saw fit to glance my way. "Who are you? Are you allowed in here right now?"

"I'm a member of the press." I even felt my shoulders sliding further back when I said it. My chin might've lifted a little, too.

"Are you, now?" He raised his camera and took a few shots before I could react.

"Hey! I didn't tell you I wanted my picture taken." I touched a self-conscious hand to my updo, hoping it hadn't fallen apart during the ride.

"I'm a member of the press," he explained with a sly smile. "I was sent here by Haute Cuisine to photograph this event."

Oh, this just kept getting better. "And I was sent by them to write about it."

"It looks like we're working together." Instead of introducing himself, the way anybody who grew up outside of a cave would, he turned around and went to the kitchen, snapping one or two shots along the way.

My mouth opened. My mouth closed.

I followed him.

"I'm Emma Harmon, by the way," I called out before pushing my way through swinging doors and walking into a nightmare. I had seen the kitchen at Mom's look busy, but nothing like this.

"Behind you!"

I jumped out of the way to avoid being run over, but then had to duck to the right to avoid a waiter carrying a tray overhead to keep it from being smashed into. It was a warzone.

Luckily, somebody spotted me from across the gleaming, white-tiled kitchen. "Emma? I don't believe it!"

The sight of Robbie—*Robert, Robert, his name is Robert*—coming to me with arms outstretched was what I'd imagine spotting an oasis in the middle of the desert would be like.

Finally, somebody I knew. I wouldn't have to feel like I had no place there.

His smile was familiar, along with the dimples in his cheeks. He always did have a baby face. I bet it didn't do him any favors when he was trying to be taken seriously as a chef.

"You look fantastic. What brings you here?" He beamed before leaning in to kiss my cheek. There was a frantic sort of energy about him, like he was hovering a few inches above the ground and ready to take off at any second.

"I'm writing about the opening! This is incredible." Funny how standing in the kitchen with the executive chef was like standing in the center of a force field. Everybody gave us a few feet of space as they practically ran from place to place, putting the finishing touches on that night's offerings.

And it smelled beyond mouthwatering. Heavenly, in fact. I could hardly believe it was my job to taste this food and describe it. Like a dream.

"You always did like to write," he nodded in approval, dark eyes twinkling. "When you were supposed to be helping me prep ingredients. How's your mom?"

That was so like him. In the middle of the biggest night of his career and he asked about my mom. We made small talk for a minute before being interrupted by a force of nature as it blew into the kitchen.

A force of nature that took the shape of a tall man with golden skin and hair, wearing a suit that looked like it might've been made especially for him. His pinkie ring flashed when he held a hand to his ear, and I realized he was talking into an earpiece.

His gaze fell on me, and in a snap, he went from a too-busy-to-care millionaire property developer to a warm, gracious host. "Hello, there. Any friend of my partner's is a friend of mine. James Flynn. And you are?"

Robbie cleared his throat. "Miss Emma Harmon is here to write about the restaurant opening for one of Haute Cuisine's publications. And she is an old friend of mine."

A silent message passed from one man to the other. They were like women, in a way. They had their own language which didn't need words to be expressed. And I didn't need to hear Robbie tell James to back off to get the message loud and clear.

James's smile never slipped. It only tightened a little. "That's great. We could use the favorable coverage."

The photographer joined us. I'd almost forgotten him in the mayhem. "Deke Bellingham," he announced, giving both of the men a firm handshake he conveniently forgot to give me. "Photographer."

"It's a pleasure." James cocked his head to the side. "Bellingham? The name sounds familiar."

"It's a common name." That was all he said.

At least I knew I wasn't the only one this Deke guy was rude to.

"Anyway," Robbie smiled down at me, "let me show you around before we get started. I want to make sure you get the full idea of the restaurant before I'm too busy to breathe, much less talk with you." He ushered me out of the kitchen, which was just fine with me since I could hardly hear myself think, and back into the cool quiet of the dining room.

"This is all so exciting," I gushed. "We're all proud of you. You've come a long way from Sweet Nothings."

"But that's where my heart is—not so much the café as the town, those memories. My heart is still in pastry and baking, even though I broadened my studies. And it was watching Sylvia manage things that led me to pursue business along with cooking. I wanted to have a place of my own one day, like she does."

Darn it if I didn't almost tear up. "She would be so happy to hear you say that. She always thought so highly of you." To the point where she went out of her way to throw us together, certain we would make an ideal couple. She hasn't changed a bit over the years.

He looked around the room, now a little busier than it had been before as servers set up stations. "I decided to serve miniature versions of the restaurant's signature dishes tonight, to allow guests the ability to move around. Here, we have the seafood station. Over there," he pointed across the room, "will be the beef and game. Poultry is the next over, and then desserts."

He lowered his voice, leaning in slightly "Can you believe my partner suggested a chocolate fountain? Where are we? A casino buffet?"

I giggled. "Hey. To some people, that's the height of sophistication." And I had never been one to turn down a chocolate fountain, no matter how bacteria-laden they were supposed to be. It was chocolate, for heaven's sake. All I could eat.

"Well, he likes to give the impression of having been born with a silver spoon, but don't let him fool you." Robbie's gaze swept over the view of the beach and the ocean beyond. The sun was starting to make up its mind that it wanted to set, casting gold and rose and orange light over the water.

He shook himself a little, and his smile reappeared. "I'd better get back to the kitchen before somebody burns the place down. Enjoy yourself tonight, all right?" I got another kiss on the cheek before he made a beeline for the kitchen.

"Does Marsha know about your relationship with Chef Robert?"

I rolled my eyes, turning to Deke with a sigh. "Does Marsha know you tend not to introduce yourself to the people you're working with? By name, I mean? Does she know you're rude?"

"Deflection." He had unusual eyes, gray flecked with gold. I always noticed eyes—the windows to the soul and all that. His narrowed. "The mark of a guilty person."

"I don't have anything to feel guilty about. Chef Robert and I knew each other a long time ago when he apprenticed for my mother. That's all."

"Hmm." That was the only response I got, but it was enough to clench my jaw tight enough to crack the crab legs at the raw bar.

I settled for taking notes on my phone, dictating softly as I walked around before the doors opened and the room flooded with people.

The party was about to begin.

CHAPTER FOUR

"Would you mind sticking close to me?" I asked Deke, catching up to him as he took photos of just about everybody in attendance. "And why are you taking so many pictures? How many do you think could possibly be printed?"

"I like photography." He looked down at the plate of appetizers I carried. "And how many of those things do you need to eat in order to write a few words about them?"

I barely kept myself from kicking him. "I like crab cakes."

"There you go. Besides, you never know when you're going to take that one, perfect shot."

"And I guess you never know when you'll find the perfect crab cake." I popped another one into my waiting mouth, savoring the flavor. Usually, crab cakes were mostly filler, in my experience, anyway. This one was chock-full of tender crab that tasted like it had been caught that very day. I made a note to address the freshness, the attention to quality.

I stumbled when Deke backed into me as he was taking a

shot. The man had no interest in anything beyond what he was doing. He'd even forgotten I was behind him.

And he'd sent me falling against a very beautiful, very annoyed woman who glared at me like I'd just kicked her dog. "Excuse you!" she snarled. She wasn't so beautiful when she snarled.

I recognized her even with that nasty expression. She was Aubrey Klein, Robbie's wife. I'd read about her during my research leading up to the event. "Mrs. Klein, excuse me. My photographer—"

"Never mind." She kept moving, storming away in her Louboutins. I normally needed Raina to explain designer names to me, but I recognized the red soles.

"Good shots," Deke muttered as he captured her furious retreat, nodding in approval of his own cleverness.

I elbowed him before I had the chance to ask myself whether it was a good idea to elbow him. "She was mad because you knocked me into her."

Blink, blink. "I did?"

"Yes! You've knocked me aside twice tonight." I paused, skeptical. "Did you really not know?"

He had the good grace to appear apologetic. "I tend to get in the zone and forget what's going on around me. I'm sorry about that." He flashed a sheepish smile that melted my icy exterior just a little. When he wasn't acting like an ignorant weirdo, he was actually pretty cute with his slightly-spiky brown hair and the sort of smile that normally put me at ease.

I nodded toward the front of the room, James and Robbie had gotten together in front of the windows looking out over the ocean. It looked like they were about to make a speech. Without hesitating, Deke took my hand and pulled me behind him, jockeying for a position among the reporters and video cameras recording for local news.

"Sorry… sorry… sorry… excuse us…" Why I felt the need to apologize and he didn't was a mystery, but I couldn't see bumping into people and not saying I was sorry. It wasn't good manners.

James spoke first, raising his champagne glass high. "Thank you all for joining us here tonight. This project has been a labor of love from the very start, and I could not imagine a better partner than the one standing beside me. Between my know-how and Chef Robert's culinary expertise, I am confident we've positioned ourselves as the ultimate luxury destination along the New Jersey coastline."

This got a great deal of applause, including from Robbie's wife who now smiled graciously as she petted her husband's arm. I couldn't help but bristle a little as I watched this—not that Robbie meant anything to me, not that he had for many years and even then, it was just a teenage crush. She struck me as fake, shallow, like this was all for show.

Maybe because she'd looked like she wanted to grind me into the sand outside the resort for jostling her. People had a tendency to show their true colors in those little moments when they thought nobody noticed.

Robbie raised his glass, too. "I can't tell you what it means to see you all here." Unlike James, whose speech rang out with a bit of showmanship, a bit of polish, Robbie was speaking from the heart. "This is the culmination of a lifelong dream, and I admit I'm a bit overwhelmed. I owe so much to my wife, Aubrey, who's stood by my side through this crazy process."

Aubrey kissed his cheek to rapturous applause. Cameras flashed, making her hair shine like copper and her gold dress sparkle and flash. She was a star tonight, and she knew it.

I had to applaud, too, but not for Aubrey. Robbie deserved this. I was so stinking proud.

Deke caught sight of my goofy smile and wisely held his tongue, choosing to do his job instead. He caught James shaking Robbie's hand, the two of them posing together, before James headed back to the kitchen. I guessed it was too busy a night to hang around making speeches for long.

I wanted to catch him, maybe get a few decent quotes for the piece which was already taking shape in my head. The entire thing couldn't be about Robbie, even if I was there technically to talk about the restaurant and the food. James was a huge part of this, the money behind the operation, and it was only right to include him.

"I'll be back," I muttered in Deke's general direction before weaving my way through the crowd.

His golden head bobbed just in front of me, leading me to the still-busy kitchen.

Only it wasn't the chatter and madness of the staff that brought me to a dead stop not two paces inside the kitchen.

It was James's voice raised in what could only be called a bark. "What are these people supposed to do?" he demanded, and something crashed to the floor. A metal bowl rolled over the tile, coming to a noisy stop.

He didn't wait for an answer. "If you can't get your act together, you're out. I don't care who you know. You are out of here!" Except for James's screaming, the kitchen had gone silent. Nobody dared move.

Except for me. I craned my neck, peering around an ice dispenser.

James had gone from tan to red, practically purple. He thrust a finger toward a man in a white jacket. "I mean it. Do you wanna leave now? You can leave now, friend, or you can speed things up and get more food out there!"

"What is this?" Robbie hurried in through another door, pushing his way through the staff who stood in mute horror and embarrassment. "What do you think you're doing, screaming at my sous chef while there's so much work to be done?"

"Maybe if your sous chef knew what he was doing, there wouldn't be empty trays out there as we speak," James spat, running hands over his head to smooth his hair into place. "Do you know how it makes us look?"

"You're making us look worse by screaming the place down back here. Do you realize you can be heard in the dining room?" Robbie was beside himself, but at least he managed to keep his voice low. "This is an embarrassment, but I don't know why I should be surprised."

He looked around. "Get to work, everyone. And see to it that the empty *platters* are replaced." He made it a point to correct his partner's misuse of the word trays.

The staff was more than happy to get back to work. Anything to get past that terribly awkward moment. I noticed the sous chef throwing a filthy look James's way, muttering something to himself as he turned back to his work.

Robbie, meanwhile, pulled James aside, which meant

they came closer to where I stood. I cowered behind the ice machine, wincing at the thought of being discovered.

"How many times do I have to remind you?" Robbie hissed. "This is my kitchen. You can be the genius behind the resort all you want, but the kitchen is my domain. Mine. Understood? That means you don't throw your temper around my kitchen, and especially not toward my staff."

"Your staff is making us look like amateurs."

"No. That would be all your doing. Get out of my face. And out of my kitchen." Robbie stalked away, past me.

He was too angry to notice I was standing there, and I silently thanked my lucky stars while wondering if everything between the two business partners was as good as they tried to make it look on the surface.

It was probably nerves over the opening. That and James seemed like a bear to work with. A man with his sort of reputation didn't get that way by being easygoing, I guessed.

I slipped from the kitchen, looking around to see if anybody lingering near the door seemed aware of what had just taken place. If they were, they'd gone back to enjoying themselves, sipping champagne and eating everything in sight. I breathed a sigh of relief for Robbie.

"Visiting your boyfriend?" I jumped a little when Deke spoke up from beside me. He had a way of sneaking up on a person.

I turned to him with a hand over my chest. "He's not my boyfriend and he never was. I don't appreciate the remarks. There was a fight in there. I was trying to get a word with James Flynn and I walked into a pretty tense situation."

"You wouldn't wanna talk about that in your piece,

though," he mused, faux-casual, examining his lens. "Wouldn't be the right look for your boyfriend."

"I swear, I will slap you," I whispered through clenched teeth as I walked away. Whether or not he heard was his business.

I pretty much stomped to the seafood table and popped a few crab cakes into my mouth because why not, then went out to the pool area to get a little air. There was a chill now, like I'd expected, and I wrapped my shawl a little tighter as I walked around and willed away the irritation mixing around with the crab in my stomach.

It was a beautiful location, for sure, and the fact that a person could walk straight from the sand to the patio surrounding the pool was nice. This stretch of beach was private, for resort guests only. I kept walking, enjoying the scent of the salt air and the crashing waves further ahead. It drew me closer.

I passed the dunes and tripped over something in the sand, then cursed myself for being so clumsy once I regained my footing. The swinging floodlights only provided so much actual light, which made walking a challenge. Especially when one didn't stop to take their heels off.

I looked down, ready to curse out whatever I had tripped over the way a person does in a situation like that.

And realized what had tripped me up.

Or, rather, who had.

"James? Mr. Flynn?" I crouched beside him, where he was sprawled on his back, half-hidden in the dune. "Mr. Flynn? Are you okay?"

That was when one of the floodlights swung in our

direction and illuminated him for a split second. But that was long enough for me to take in everything.

Wide eyes, staring at the starry sky.

Blood trickling from his mouth.

And the shiny butcher's knife sticking out of his chest. I reached for it before I could stop myself, grasping the handle like there was anything I could do for the guy. But that was what a person did when they were in a situation like that, right? They tried to help, even when it made no sense.

"Emma?"

My head snapped around at the sound of Deke's voice. His eyes were just as wide as the dead man's as he took in the sight of me grasping the handle of the murder weapon.

He looked from the knife to me. "What have you done?"

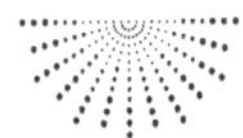

CHAPTER FIVE

"I didn't kill him." I glanced at Deke, catching him from the corner of my eye. "I didn't."

We sat side-by-side against the wall in molded plastic chairs. I still had sand stuck between my feet and my shoes. Somebody had cranked up the air conditioning to the point where I felt like I was in a fridge. Or maybe that was just me, frozen inside after what I'd discovered.

I pulled my shawl around me, like that would help. Deke finally noticed how I shivered and removed his suit jacket. "Here," he offered, draping it over my shoulders.

"For the record, I don't think you did it. You don't have to explain yourself to me." He looked around us. "Save it for the cops."

The cops. Because we were in a police station, after all.

Nobody had talked to us yet, but I had the feeling that would change soon enough. There was a ton of information for them to process, and probably a million people to question. Deke's jacket helped, but that was maybe the only positive aspect of the situation so far.

"Tell me again. What happened?" he murmured, always watching the cops and detectives who hurried around.

"I told you. I walked out onto the sand because somebody was on my last nerve and wanted to get some air. I tripped over him. This all happened maybe ten seconds before you showed up. He was just lying there, staring up at the sky."

"And you didn't see anybody?"

"No. It was dark. I didn't even see him before I tripped. But no, there was nobody. Not even on the patio. Maybe it was too chilly, I don't know."

"That's a shame." When I turned to look at him, he shrugged. "Witnesses. No witnesses."

"It must've happened right before I got there, right? He was just in the kitchen now a few minutes before then. Making a scene." I elbowed Deke. Hard. "Making a scene!"

"Ow."

"He made a big scene in there," I whispered. "He was freaking out. Anybody would've been pretty mad at him after that. I'm telling you, I got a bad feeling when I was in there."

"It's easy to say that now."

"I thought it then, too. Remember? Before you got all sarcastic with me? I told you there was a fight. It was tense. I told you so."

"Okay, okay, there was a fight. Between him and Chef Robert, right?"

Whoops. That didn't sound good for Robbie. "Yeah. I mean, James was screaming his head off at the entire kitchen staff before that. So everybody was upset. Especially the sous chef."

"Well, the cops will figure it out. That's what they do."

"Yeah, but what if—"

He looked at me. "What if what?"

I couldn't speak. Not when a certain tall, striking older man stepped into the police station and started asking questions of the front desk cop. I didn't have to hear his voice to know how it sounded. Deep, rumbling, assertive. The sort of voice a person didn't ignore unless they wanted to get grounded.

If they happened to be the man's daughter. Which I was.

"Who is that?" Deke asked, following my gaze.

"My father."

"Your father? You called your father?"

I glared at him. "Why not? Is that so bizarre?"

"How old are you?"

I wanted to kick him. So help me. "He's a detective, genius. In Cape Hope. I wanted him here for moral support and to maybe speak up on my behalf. I don't know." I shrugged. "It was the first thing that came to mind."

"I see. That makes sense."

"Thanks for the approval."

"I'm trying to be nice."

"It's a shame you have to try. It really is." I stood when my father approached, taking his usual giant strides. He was the sort of guy people got out of the way for.

"Baby." He enfolded me in his arms in a brief, tight hug. "You okay?"

"Fine. I'm not the one who had a knife sticking out of their chest." I tried to sound cheerful but failed miserably.

"Who's this guy?" He was never one for sugarcoating

things, my dad. Especially not when his daughter had discovered a dead body.

"Deke Bellingham," I explained. "The photographer I was working with tonight. He came with me for moral support. And, you know, he discovered me discovering the body, so…"

"They asked me to come." He stood, shaking Dad's hand.

"Detective George Harmon."

I wondered if he would give Deke his resume next.

He returned his attention to me, his bushy eyebrows drawing together. "Don't worry about a thing. They'll ask you a few questions, but don't let them rattle you. Okay?"

"Should I have a lawyer with me? It seems I should have a lawyer. They always have lawyers on TV."

He snickered. "This isn't TV, baby. And you're innocent. You have nothing to worry about."

He was right, obviously. I hadn't killed anybody. If I managed to let Landon get off with nothing but a lot of screaming and maybe a thrown coffee cup—it was sort of a blur—I certainly wasn't going to kill James Flynn.

Deke offered to get coffee, leaving me alone with my dad. I sat, but he chose to stand. It was easier for him to be intimidating that way, even if he didn't consciously intend to be.

"I wonder where Robbie is," I mused.

"Robbie?"

"Robert Klein. Remember? He was Mom's apprentice. It was his restaurant opening tonight."

Understanding dawned. "Oh, right. Nice kid."

"James Flynn was his business partner."

Just like that, the clouds descended again and he looked confused. "James Flynn?"

"The dead guy."

"It was James Flynn who got killed tonight?"

"Yeah. I didn't know you were familiar with him."

"Plenty of people are. He owns—owned—property in Cape Hope, too."

"I didn't know that. Well, he was pretty wealthy and connected."

"Yes, he was." Why did he sound suspicious? Deke showed up with coffee before I had the chance to ask.

"Wow, real coffee from a police station?" I asked with a grateful smile.

"No, there's a shop two doors down," he explained, offering my dad a cup which he took with a grunt of thanks.

"Extra sugar, like I asked?"

He provided a handful of sugar packets from his pants pocket. Something told me, based on his smirk, that if my father wasn't there he would've had an unwelcome opinion on my sugar habit.

A plainclothes cop approached just as I finished stirring in the last packet. "I assume you're Emma Harmon, not these two," he grunted, looking down at a sheet on a clipboard and nodded to Dad and Deke.

"That's right." My stomach turned to ice all of a sudden, and I couldn't understand why. I hadn't killed anybody. I just happened to be the idiot who tripped over the body.

The cop glanced at me. "Okay. In here." He pointed to what was little more than a cubby, the door open to reveal how cramped the room was. A metal table, three chairs. Nothing more.

I wondered how many perps had been questioned in there. How many cold-blooded killers. And here I was, about to be questioned in there, too.

Was I morbid for being slightly excited? Or was it just the fact that my Criminal Justice minor was about to be put to use for the first time since graduation? I stood on shaky legs, then had a second thought. "Can my dad come in?"

"Your dad?" The cop looked Dad up and down.

"Detective George Harmon." Dad handed the cop a business card which he perused before tucking it into a pocket of his extremely well-fitting dress slacks. Yes, the last thing I needed to be thinking about was how well this cop's pants fit, but I'd just found my first dead body. My brain needed other things to focus on for a second.

"I'm Detective Joe Sullivan." He shook Dad's hand before nodding to Deke, then to me. "This way, Miss Harmon. I guess your father can join us for this preliminary questioning, so long as he promises to leave the work to me."

Gulp.

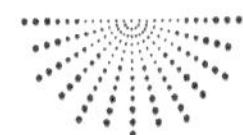

CHAPTER SIX

"Preliminary?" I asked, glancing up at Dad before following the detective to the interrogation room.

"We don't have all our ducks in a row yet, so to speak." Joe took a seat at the table, hands folded on top. Nice hands. I was always a sucker for hands. No ring. Interesting.

Get it together, Emma. This was not the time to go shopping for a Landon replacement.

"All right, Miss Harmon. Help me understand." His eyes (jade green under sooty lashes and heavy brows, it wasn't fair for a boy to have such nice eyes) narrowed as he studied what I guessed was a set of notes taken during my first statement, on the beach.

"Whatever I can do," I promised with a glance at my dad, whose face was unfortunately expressionless. I needed to know I was doing the right thing.

"You were at the event because..." Joe looked up at me, waiting.

"Like I said, I was there to write about the opening." I nodded to the notes. "It should be there."

"Emma," Dad whispered.

"No, it's all right." Joe stared at me. "Please answer my questions without additional commentary, Miss Harmon. This isn't my first questioning. You were there for work, then. Did you have a personal relationship with anyone present?"

I wished I didn't have a habit of blushing whenever somebody chastised me. I used to do it in school and it never went away. "Yes. Chef Robbie—Robert," I corrected myself, blushing harder. "We knew each other a long time ago."

"And the nature of that relationship?"

"He worked for my mother, and so did I. One summer. Him, not me. I've always worked at the café, off and on. I hadn't seen him since then, not until tonight." I also had a tendency to talk too much when I was nervous.

"And you were out on the beach because…?" He glanced up again, and I noticed how tired his voice was. How much of this had he already done that night?

"Because I needed a breath of air. It was crowded in there, so many people."

"And how did you happen upon the body?"

"I tripped over his leg." I looked to Dad again, shrugging. "It was dark out there."

"You didn't see a body lying in the sand?" Joe asked with a smirk.

"It was dark," I repeated. "And I wasn't expecting a body to be lying in my path."

"*Emma.*" He didn't whisper this time. Dad's voice was tight.

"You make a habit of walking alone on the beach in the dark?" Joe asked, brows lifting.

"Detective, I apologize for my daughter's attitude, and she ought to know better, having studied Criminal Justice," Dad muttered in a gruff voice. "But certainly, she can't be blamed for walking along the beach."

"When she was supposed to be working?" Joe countered, one corner of his generous mouth screwing up in a smirk. "I'll grant you that one. But what about her fingerprints on the murder weapon?"

"Her what on the what now?" Dad turned in his chair, facing me head-on. "What is he saying?"

"Not a bright move for a Criminal Justice major," Joe muttered under his breath.

"Minor," I corrected before answering Dad. "It was just one of those things. I know it didn't make any sense, but I thought maybe I could help him. I wasn't thinking."

"You touched the murder weapon? You know better than that!"

"Is this not the first time you've been in the presence of a murder weapon?" Joe asked. I thought he might've been amused by this, but he wasn't smiling.

"I've taught her better," Dad growled. "We've talked about analyzing crime scenes since she was a little girl."

"Sounds like a happy childhood," Joe observed.

"Detective—" Dad was halfway out of his seat. I tugged on his sleeve and shook my head. It wasn't worth it.

I turned back to the detective then. "You know, there are plenty of other people you might want to be talking to right now, rather than wasting time being snarky toward an innocent person."

"Snarky?" Joe snickered. "Who should I be talking to, in your learned opinion?" He leaned back in his chair, grinning.

"Try everybody who works in the kitchen, for one thing. There was a big blow-up in there not ten minutes before I tripped over James's body. He was screaming at the sous chef, making a big deal out of a few empty platters in the dining room. Robbie said he could be heard out there, among the guests."

"Robbie?" A brow lifted.

"You know who I mean. The sous chef was probably humiliated by that. And Robbie warned James to mind his business and stay out of the kitchen. James stormed away. Anybody could've followed him."

"Somebody did," Joe agreed. "And they just so happened to sink one of Chef Robert Klein's signature engraved knives into his chest. Right after, as you just told me, Chef Robert warned Mr. Flynn to mind his business."

Oh, no. My heart sank when I realized I'd basically just set the scene for Robbie to have murdered James. Dad whispered something under his breath that sounded suspiciously like a swear word.

"I would suggest you don't leave town, Miss Harmon," Detective Joe warned as he stood. "I'll most likely be calling tomorrow to have you return for more questioning."

"More?" I asked. "I can't stay in town. I'm not from here. I live in Cape Hope, I hadn't intended to spend the night. It's not like my job will pay for this."

He lifted his broad shoulders. "That isn't my problem, is it? Not when your fingerprints are on the murder weapon."

Dad took my arm. "I'll put you up for the night, doll. You don't have to worry about it."

I still had so many questions, protestations. Not to mention wanting to tell Detective Joe where he could get off with his snarky comments. But Dad made a point of pulling me out of my chair and leading me out of the room before I could say anything to further embarrass myself.

Meanwhile, to my surprise—it shouldn't have come as a surprise, not really—Deke emerged from the next room over, and the young woman who followed him was carrying a clipboard like Joe's. Of course, they'd want to walk to Deke, since he was the one who found me finding James.

"Everything okay?" he asked, looking from Dad to me.

Dad only snorted his response.

"Define okay," I whispered. "No, I don't think so. I think they really believe I had something to do with it."

"Don't say that," Dad warned. "Let's get out of here. The walls always have ears."

"Remember!" Joe called out behind us. "Stay in town, Emma. I'll want to talk to you again."

"Lucky me," I whispered as Dad steered me from the station with Deke bringing up the rear.

"You could've done better in there, sweetheart." Dad was fit to be tied, and probably only Deke's presence kept him from chewing me out. I never thought I'd be glad to have an obnoxious photographer around.

"I'm sorry, Dad. My mouth got away from me. But honestly, I didn't do it. I didn't even have a drop of blood on me, and there was no motive. James seemed like a real jerk, but I didn't have any reason to kill him."

"No, but…" He glanced at Deke and decided to hold his

tongue. "We'd better get you a room for the night. I know how these guys work. He'll probably want you back first thing in the morning after getting forensics reports."

"I have a room in town," Deke offered. "Not that I intended to share, mind you, but I'll be here. In case you need any moral support." He handed me a business card, and I wondered how many people still carried them. That was the second one I'd seen that night.

I accepted it gratefully anyway. "Thank you. I'll call you in the morning, for sure." Maybe he wasn't the most terrible person in the world, especially if he'd defended me to the police. I hoped he did.

He'd better have.

"Oh! Your jacket!" I dashed after him, sliding it from my shoulders. "Thank you again."

He took it with that same boyish, sheepish smile I'd seen earlier in the night. "No problem. Try to get some sleep tonight, okay? It'll be all right. Everything will."

I wondered what made him such an expert and decided not to ask. It would be better to believe without asking.

"Emma?" Dad was waiting, hands thrust into his jacket pockets. He eyed Deke with roughly the same level of suspicion a canary would give a cat. I hurried back to him and accepted the arm he wrapped around my shoulders in a protective manner.

I finally felt safe, for the first time all night.

What a shame it wouldn't last forever.

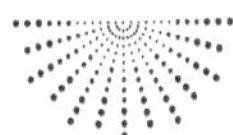

CHAPTER SEVEN

It was the knocking that woke me up. The incessant pounding, like the person on the other side of the door would break it down if I didn't open up.

What time was it? I fumbled around for my phone but couldn't find it in the mess that was my bed. I hadn't had a restful night, to put it mildly.

"Em! It's me. Open up before I have the hotel do it!"

Raina's voice finally worked its way through my awareness. Raina! What was she doing there? Only curiosity could've gotten me out of bed in the middle of the night.

Only it wasn't the middle of the night. I had drawn the drapes before collapsing into bed, but light managed to sneak through around the edges. And my best friend was going to get me thrown out of the hotel if she didn't stop making a commotion out in the hall.

"Hang on!" I managed to call out as I scrambled up and across the room with a sheet wrapped around my underwear-clad body.

She burst in like a breath of spring, but that was always her way. She managed to light up any room she entered. "This is an absolute outrage," she announced as she threw open the curtains. "How anybody could even associate you with the word murder is beyond me. If you didn't murder Landon—or at least cut off something vital—why would you murder a perfect stranger?"

I could hardly remember filling her in on any of the details, but I guessed I must have. "I suppose they'll have it pretty much figured out by now. They must. Right?" I stopped short of crawling back into bed, settling for sitting with a pillow held tight in my arms and wishing my head was on it and I was sleeping.

This was quite a reversal. Usually, Raina was the one getting dragged out of sleep by me.

She whirled on me, dark hair swinging over her shoulders. "I brought reinforcements." She dumped a bag onto the bed, sending clothes and toiletries pouring out.

"Bless you," I groaned. "I was wondering what I was supposed to do today. I don't think a second visit to the police station classifies as a Little Black Dress occasion."

"A waste of time." She flopped into an armchair, crossing her legs while removing her sunglasses. She might just as easily have flown in from Milan or Paris, she was so effortlessly chic.

"Speaking of a waste of time, I can't believe you drove all the way down from Manhattan!"

"That was not a waste, my dear. Not when my best friend is a murder suspect."

"I don't think I'm a suspect. Not really. But maybe. I don't know." I held my head in my hands, sure it would pop off if I didn't keep it in place. "I can't stop thinking of that man's eyes, staring. Wide open. And the blood. He was just alive, you know? Like only a few minutes earlier. I saw him, I heard him."

"Heard him fighting with First Kiss Robbie."

"Please, let's not call him that right now. I'll probably be talking about him with Detective Joe and don't wanna slip up. He already thinks I'm ridiculous."

"He should stop wasting time with you, then, if that's what he thinks."

"I found the body. I touched the handle of the knife. Of course, he's going to want to talk to me. I need to put my criminal justice hat on and think it through from his perspective."

"First, I think you need to shower and dress and come out with me for some breakfast and coffee. You'll think better on a full stomach. You always do." Years of being college roommates and best friends gave her that level of insight.

I did as I was told, since it was easier to follow instructions in situations like this. Poor Robbie. After all that hard work and all his dreams, it had fallen apart like this. He had to be devastated. What would become of their big project with one of the major players in the morgue?

He hadn't done it. He couldn't have. Robbie didn't possess a violent bone. Not even a violent blood cell. He was one of the kindest, sweetest people in the world.

He didn't sound so kind or sweet last night. I paused in the act of shampooing my hair, staring at the tile wall in front of me. That was true, wasn't it? Well, he needed to know when to bring the hammer down, and James had been sticking his nose where it didn't belong.

How often had that been the case? And how tired might Robbie have been of his business partner's interference?

I couldn't believe it. Was I honestly making a case in my head for Robbie being the murderer? First Kiss Robbie?

I dipped beneath the hot, steamy spray and pushed these thoughts away. There had to be another explanation. I willed the water to wash away my doubts and send them down the drain.

If only it were that simple.

By the time I finished washing, drying and dressing, I'd missed three phone calls.

"It's your mom," Raina murmured, her hand over the microphone. "I didn't want to pick up but she keeps calling."

I drew a deep breath and braced myself before holding out my hand. I got no further than, "Mom?" before the tirade began.

"How could they think you would be responsible for a murder?" she demanded. "Who are these chuckleheads? Did they even attend the academy?"

"Mom—"

"Your father called and told me, and let me tell you that was not an easy conversation."

"Mom?"

"And I heard *her* talking in the background as if she has any say in any of this, as if she even deserves to speak your name or feign concern."

"Mom!" I finally had to raise my voice. "I'm okay. I don't think they suspect me, I really don't." I held up my crossed fingers with a shrug, and Raina merely shook her head with a look of disapproval. Not because I was sorta-kinda lying to my mom, but because she didn't approve of anybody considering me a murder suspect. "This is all very confusing and I'll probably hear more about it today, and I promise I'll keep you posted."

"That vile detective will allow you to come home, won't he?"

I bit my lip. That, I couldn't lie about so easily. "I don't know."

"You don't?"

"I have to talk to him, don't I? At most, I'm a person of interest. So long as I promise not to leave the state, I should be good." Now I was pulling things out of thin air. Anything to calm her down. It sounded reasonable enough.

"You need to be home at a time like this."

"I heartily agree. But Raina's here, she brought me clothes and whatnot, and we're going to get breakfast now. I'll keep you posted, like I said. I promise."

Just before we ended the call, something occurred to me. "Mom! Hang on. I need your promise. Your heartfelt, absolute, hundred-percent promise."

"Anything, honey. You know that."

"Don't breathe a word of this to anybody else. Darcy, okay. But that's it. Nobody. I don't want to come back to town and face a thousand questions. You know how people can be."

Mom sniffed. "Emma Harmon, sometimes I think you have no faith in me."

I let that one slide. Raina was giggling by the time I tossed the phone aside. "She's a piece of work. I love her."

"Me, too," I muttered with a roll of my eyes. "Come on.

There's a cup of coffee somewhere with my name on it. A very large, very strong cup."

We didn't get more than ten feet down the hall before my phone rang yet again. I didn't recognize the number, but it was local to the area. "Looks like we might have to put a hold on breakfast," I whispered before answering.

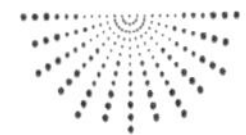

"This is absolutely ridiculous. Emma ought to have her lawyer here if you're going to question her like she's a common criminal."

Joe blinked, looking from Raina to me. "Who's this again?"

"A friend of mine. She came down when she heard what happened."

"And brought clothes," he noted as he looked over his notes. "A shame. That was a cute dress."

"Funny," I murmured, though I couldn't help wondering if he was making fun of me or actually complimenting my outfit from the night before. I then noticed that he was wearing the same burgundy shirt and grey tie as he'd worn when we first spoke. I softened, but only slightly.

He looked up at Raina with a sigh. "If Miss Harmon needed her lawyer, I would let her know. At this time, she is a person of interest in the case. We aren't charging her with anything. If at any point she feels uncomfortable with the direction the questions take, she has every right to request a lawyer. Does that satisfy you, Miss…?"

"Delancey. Raina Delancey."

He smirked. "Sure. Delancey. The Manhattan real estate family."

"We were, once," she allowed. "My father sold his interests years ago."

"I'm sure that was plenty of interest," he observed, and I practically heard the wheels turning in his head as he took in the designer sunglasses perched on top of her head, the Birkin bag, the cashmere shawl draped around her shoulders.

He would be making a mistake if he wrote her off as an airheaded, spoiled rich kid. She had more smarts in her pinky than most people had in their whole body.

"I think we were talking about the case?" I asked, steering things back to me. It wasn't eagerness to solve the case that drove me. It was an empty stomach.

Joe cleared his throat. "Right. The initial reports came in overnight. A single blow, straight to the heart. Killed him instantly. No time to scream or fight back. Whoever did this was no stranger. Or, if they were, they did not give the appearance of having an intent to harm Mr. Flynn."

"What makes you say that?" Raina asked.

I answered. "Because whoever it was got close enough to pull a knife and sink it into his chest without him fighting back first."

The room fell silent.

Gulp. I glanced at Joe with a shrug. "I would assume, anyway."

His eyes narrowed as he regarded me. "Yes. That is the

theory we're working with. Interesting, the way it fell from your lips without any effort."

"It's common sense. Besides, I—"

"Studied Criminal Justice and spent evening suppers discussing the grisly details of your father's cases. I know, I know." He shook his head as he looked over his notes. "Help me work out a timeline, if you would. From what I can tell so far, you're the only person who both witnessed the fight in the kitchen and stumbled over the body. Try to be as specific as you can. How much time passed between the fight and your walk along the beach?"

Dang it. I closed my eyes, taking a few deep breaths to center myself. I hadn't been paying attention to the time while in the moment. After all, how was I supposed to know James would end up dead and therefore everything would be considered important later on?

"Let's see. I slipped out of the kitchen—"

"Slipped out?"

I frowned, opening one eye. "Yes. I wasn't exactly trying to let everybody know I overheard what went on."

"So, wait. You were hiding in the kitchen?"

"No. I mean. Not really. I went in because I was following James Flynn, trying to get a few words with him for my article. By the time I caught up with him, he was already on a tirade. I was embarrassed for everybody in the kitchen and knew I shouldn't technically be listening, so…"

"Instead of leaving the kitchen, you hid."

I sighed, eyes wide open now. "You asked me to give you a timeline, right? I'm trying to. Yes, I'm a Very Bad Girl for listening when I should've ducked out. I'll write it out fifty times if it makes you feel better."

He scowled. "Go on."

I closed my eyes again. "Anyway. He was yelling and berating the sous chef and generally everybody else along with him. Robb—Chef Robert came in and told everybody to get back to work. I took it as him sticking up for his people. He didn't want James—"

"Please, spare me the analysis of motive," Joe warned. "I'm not interested in that. I want the timing. What happened next?"

I gritted my teeth but managed to hold back a snide comment. "Then, Robbie pulled James aside. They were closer to me at that point. I was hiding next to the ice machine." My cheeks. How they burned with shame.

"Mm-hmm."

My eyes were closed but I would've bet good money on the detective smirking in a know-it-all way.

"Robert told James to stay out of the kitchen. He'd warned him about it before, he said. While he was in front of the staff, too, he made a comment about not being surprised that James would make them look unprofessional."

"Did he explain that?"

"No. He didn't explain it when they were away from the rest of the staff, either. He only told James to stay out of the kitchen and take care of the resort. Then, he walked away, past me. I remember being glad he didn't see me."

"Who walked away?"

"Robert. When he did, I backed out of the kitchen. I was glad to be out of there. It was one of those really icky situations." I opened my eyes to find Joe staring at me and oh, boy, did I wish he wouldn't look at me with those eyes of his. It was unnerving, and not in an entirely bad way.

"Icky situations. Yes, I guess it would be icky." He snickered to himself as he made a note. "Then what?"

"I spoke with Deke outside the kitchen doors, told him some of what happened—that there'd been a fight, I don't think I got too far into it—then walked through the room and outside, to the pool."

"Why?"

"Because I wanted some air." And Deke had been insulting.

"Approximately how much time passed between the scene in the kitchen and the point where you stumbled over the body?"

"I can't say with complete accuracy, but five to ten minutes. He must have gone outside to get some air, too, and somebody followed him out."

"Please, Miss Harmon. Again with the supposition. I don't need to hear your take on it, only the facts."

"Well, I'm sorry, but I didn't time myself. I'm only trying to help."

"I don't need your help."

"Then why am I here, if you don't need my help?"

He blew out a long sigh. "You are not here to help me solve this. You are here to provide information. Facts. Nothing more."

"You should be questioning that sous chef," Raina suggested, arms folded. She started jigging her foot back and forth, which meant she was good and irritated.

"Thank you for your expert opinion, but we have that

under control." He looked back to me. "And why, again, are your fingerprints on the murder weapon?"

"I reacted without thinking."

"I find it hard to believe." He smirked.

Hot or not, I was getting tired of his attitude. "Unless you're going to charge me with a crime, I see no reason to stay here and get insulted."

Whoa. Had I really just said that? Was I trying to get myself in trouble? Everybody knew only guilty people said things like that. Or red herrings on TV police procedurals. I wasn't trying to be either of those.

I continued to babble. "Everything you have against me is circumstantial, so I can't imagine being considered a suspect. I've told you everything I can about what happened last night. I wish it had been anybody but me who'd found the body, since I could be home right now rather than sitting here."

"You wouldn't even try to speak up on an old friend's behalf? I find that hard to believe."

I froze. "Huh? You can't think…"

"As of this moment, Miss Harmon, Robert Klein is our prime suspect. Thanks to the information which you've provided regarding the argument he and Mr. Flynn engaged in minutes before the murder, to say nothing of his finger-prints on the murder weapon and the fact that no one can account for his whereabouts after the argument you over-heard, I'm confident I have enough for an arrest."

My mouth fell open. Tears blurred my vision. No. It couldn't be.

Had I just signed First Kiss Robbie's arrest warrant?

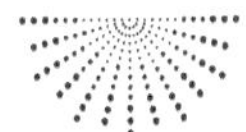

A knock at the door broke the heavy silence.

"Detective? I have a gentleman out here who says you're questioning his daughter?"

Dad. I had never been so glad to know he was around.

Joe, however, did not appear to share my enthusiasm. "I should've known. Do you always travel with an entourage, Miss Harmon?"

"Only when I find dead bodies," I smiled sweetly. I was still reeling from the news about Robbie, but I could still be sarcastic.

"I'd say we're finished here, anyway," Raina decided, standing. "If anything, this has been a waste of time for everyone involved. She didn't tell you anything you didn't already know, and all you've done is insult her."

"Please, Miss Delancey, I've had about enough." He loosened his necktie with a sigh. "I don't know about either of you, but I haven't been home since I started my shift yesterday afternoon. When a man as prominent as James

Flynn is murdered, people want answers. I'm only doing my job."

For a second—just the splittest of split seconds—I felt sorry for him. I truly did. "If there's anything else I can provide, please let me know," I offered, contrite, before reminding myself that this creep wanted to arrest Robbie.

He inclined his head toward me. "You can stay here in town, since you're still a person of interest in the case."

"Anything but that."

Dad entered the room, clearly unable to wait. "My daughter will return home today," he announced.

"Pardon me?" Joe's eyebrows almost left his head, they jumped so high.

"Call it a professional courtesy, Detective. She's no more than a half-hour down the road should you need her, and I'll vouch for her whereabouts. She won't be leaving the state any time soon. There is no reason for her to live in a hotel room when we both know she didn't kill that man."

"You might think you know, but I never said I did," Joe reminded him. "It could be that she was angry on behalf of an old friend."

Even I had to laugh at that. "Come, now. You can't believe that."

"Can't I?" he challenged, holding my gaze for a long moment. "I don't know."

"You're right. You don't know." Dad's arm landed over my shoulders. "As I said, call it a professional courtesy, Detective. I would be most appreciative. You know our departments have worked together in the past."

Joe nodded, though he was frowning. "Yes. I know. Very well. Miss Harmon, I would advise you leave the investigating to the professionals. I'll give you a call if I need anything further from you."

"What gives you the idea that I would try to investigate?" I couldn't help but ask.

He grinned. "Call it a hunch."

I was never so glad to leave any place in all my life. Even so, I couldn't help but imagine Robbie. What was he going through?

"Do you think the police are at his house?" I asked Dad as we descended the steps in front of the station. "Maybe they're going through his things and questioning him? Or maybe they're at the restaurant, and he's with them, and they're peppering him with accusations. Oh, jeez, I feel awful. This is all my fault!"

"Your fault?" Dad came to a stop when we reached the sidewalk. "What makes you say that?"

"If I hadn't gone and told them about the argument with James, they wouldn't consider him the prime suspect. That detective said he's going to arrest Robbie for this!"

Dad patted my back. "You're going to have to let the police do their job, kiddo."

I looked up at him like he'd just started speaking in tongues. "No way. No. I won't. Not if doing their jobs means charging Robbie with this. They can't do that!"

"Honey, if they have the evidence…"

"Oh, for Pete's sake!" I threw my hands into the air. "According to the evidence, I'm a suspect because my fingerprints were on the knife. That doesn't mean I killed him. This is all specious at best."

"If you had pursued a career with the police department, maybe you could do something about this."

Not this again. "Dad. Now's not the time to lecture me on my career. I know I can help Robbie. I just need the chance."

He looked pained, his brows drawing together the way they normally did when he had a headache. "Don't make me regret promising you'd behave yourself."

"You didn't promise."

"No, not in so many words, but my butt's on the line if you start trouble. Do you understand?" No matter how old I got, there would never be a time when my father couldn't bring me to heel when he took that tone.

"Yes," I sighed, looking at the sidewalk.

He kissed the top of my head. "And you'll go straight home after getting your things from the hotel?"

"Yes."

"Okay." He made a move like he was about to go to his car, then paused. "By the way, if it makes you feel any better, once the police start looking into James Flynn's business interests, they'll have more than a few suspects to choose from. I wouldn't start mourning for Robert yet if I were you."

Well.

If the man wanted to dissuade me from getting myself involved, he shouldn't have said that. My head snapped up. "What's that mean?"

His brows drew closer together, until they became a unibrow. "I shouldn't have said anything. When will I learn?"

"No, Daddy. Come on. Tell me!" I trotted behind him as he walked to his truck, and Raina trotted behind me. "Please? You can't leave me hanging like that!"

"Leave it to the police, doll." He looked to Raina before climbing into the truck. "See if you can keep her out of trouble?"

"I can't make any promises," she said with a laugh. "But I'll do my best."

"I'll catch up with you later," Dad promised before closing the door.

I watched with a sinking heart as he pulled away from the curb.

"So?" Raina asked. "Are you gonna be a good girl and go home like your dad asked?"

I gave her a look. "What do you think?"

"Good. I was just checking." She watched as I pulled my phone from my purse. "Who are you calling?"

"Deke. He took pictures of everything last night. I mean everything. He must've seen something. Besides, I wanna tell him I'm going home." I dialed his number and waited.

"Hmm," Raina murmured. "Is he tall? Brown hair? Sort of sexy but in an offbeat way?"

"Sexy?" I snickered. "I wouldn't call him sexy. Cute, maybe. But I was too busy trying not to kick him most of the time to notice. Why?"

When I stopped speaking, I noticed the sound of a ringing phone coming from just behind me.

Raina's eyes were wide. "Because he's standing behind you. Why do you think I was able to describe him?"

Dang it.

I turned slowly, lowering the phone. "Hi," I smiled. "Good morning."

He slid his phone into his pocket. "Good morning." Whether he heard my comment or not was a mystery.

With the way my luck was running, he'd heard every word.

"I was just calling you to say I'm going home. My dad convinced the detective to let me leave town."

"I see. Where is home?"

"Cape Hope. So. Not far. No reason for me to stay here when I could just drive up if need be. Or somebody could drive down." And there I went again, talking nonstop because I was embarrassed. Even worse than that, now that Raina had described Deke as sexy, I couldn't stop looking at him that way.

And I saw that she had a point. He wore a white shirt, the top two buttons open to reveal tanned skin and the barest hint of a firm chest. Slim waist and hips leading to a pair of jeans he was wearing the living heck out of.

"Thanks for thinking of calling to let me know," he said. "I'm here to pick up my memory card."

"Oh? So they wanted to look at the pictures you took?"

"Right. I don't usually hand those over for anything, but…" He shrugged. "What are you gonna do?"

I chewed my lip. Should I ask? Should I not ask? We hadn't exactly gotten off on the best foot and he had just overheard me saying I wanted to kick him. The odds weren't exactly in my favor. But I would question myself endlessly if I didn't at least try.

"You think there might be any chance of my taking a look at what you have? I mean, uh, on your memory card. The pictures."

"In case you're looking for the foot that fell out of your mouth, I think it's around here somewhere…" Raina whispered.

I hoped he couldn't hear her. It was bad enough I was blushing hard enough to hurt.

He kept a straight face, at least. "Sure. I had planned to go over them with a fine-toothed comb, myself. It isn't every night I come across a woman I'm supposed to be working with as she discovers a dead body."

"I'm glad I helped keep things interesting, anyway."

"You said you're going home? Why don't I drive down tomorrow? I have a few things to take care of today and had planned on driving home, or else I'd suggest meeting up later on."

I wondered what he could possibly have to do that was anything nearly as important as this, but for once, I stopped myself before my mouth got the better of me. He didn't know Robbie from Adam. He had nothing personal riding on this.

He hadn't all but pointed the finger at an old friend.

Just the same, I bristled. "Yeah. I guess tomorrow will work. They won't put anybody in the electric chair between now and then."

Raina clicked her tongue in disapproval, but I didn't much care. At least, I told myself I didn't.

"I don't think they use the electric chair anymore," Deke mused aloud before turning to Raina. "Deke Bellingham, by the way."

"Oh, hello. I think we've met before, actually. Raina Delancey."

"Sure! How are you?" He actually smiled at her, too. A real, genuine smile. No sarcasm detected.

And for the briefest moment, I felt a pang of jealousy I couldn't understand while they exchanged pleasantries.

He remembered I was there before long, however. "Okay, so I'll give you a call tomorrow? We can make plans."

"Yeah. Sure."

But he was already halfway down the sidewalk. That was more the Deke I had come to know.

"Do you know who that is?" Raina whispered when we were alone again.

"No, but you clearly do."

She waved a hand. "Sure, I've run into him once or twice. Deacon Bellingham. Bellingham Candy. They make the—"

"I know the name," I marveled, watching Deke jog up the stairs and into the station. I'd been eating his grandfather's candy since I had teeth. "He's gotta be worth millions."

"Tens of millions," Raina marveled. "What's he doing taking pictures for Haute Cuisine?"

I intended to find out.

CHAPTER TEN

"This is just terrible. I can't imagine. Robbie? Who would ever suspect Robbie of such a thing?"

"If you don't stop shaking your head that way, you're going to have a terrible crick in your neck," I warned from my stool in the kitchen, where I frosted cupcakes. I had to do something, and sitting alone in my apartment certainly wasn't helping anything.

Mom picked up a tray of fresh carrot cake squares with cream cheese frosting which I had just finished decorating. "I would think you'd be a bit more concerned. He was your first love, after all."

She was out the swinging door before I processed what she'd said. "Wait, what?" I called out, following her with the offset spatula in hand. "He was no such thing!"

There were a few people scattered around the café, drinking coffee and enjoying books from next door. All of them looked up at once.

I waved the spatula. "Sorry to disturb you," I murmured before glaring at my mother.

"Well? Isn't that how it was?" She seemed to have no trouble discussing anything personally related to me while in the presence of her customers.

"No. That's not how it was. And for the love of everything, don't go spreading that around. It's bad enough you already told people about what happened last night when I expressly asked you not to. Maybe I should start encouraging you to spread news around. Maybe then, you won't."

"Oh, for heaven's sake. You're making a big deal out of nothing. So I told Trixie and Nell. What's the big deal?"

I winced. "Trixie Graham who writes for the *Cape Hope Times*? Holy jeez, Mom!"

"Trixie Graham who happens to be a close, personal friend of mine." True, Trixie had kept the café's name in the paper in the months after its opening, casually mentioning it from time to time in her "local interest" articles. She and Mom had been thick as thieves from that point on.

Rather than remind my mother of the line between trusting a friend and keeping in mind what that friend did for a living, I returned to the kitchen and got back to frosting my cupcakes.

I might have stress-eaten one in the process.

Why did it feel like every time I had my life under control, it spiraled further out of my grasp? I'd scratched and clawed and turned my blog into a profitable business which had parlayed itself into a chance to write for Haute Cuisine.

Only to find my boyfriend in bed with a bimbo.

I'd gone on my first assignment, planning to wow my editor while supporting an old friend.

Only to discover a dead body and maybe-kinda-sorta get my old friend accused of murder.

And there was no chance in heck of keeping the news from spreading. Not with Mom using my personal life as a point of interest. And especially not since she knew Robbie personally, and as such could claim personal bereavement at his being accused of the crime.

I could glue her mouth shut, but anything short of that would be a useless endeavor.

I considered a second cupcake, but the back door opened to reveal my sister before I had the chance.

"I wanted to pop over since I heard you were here," she whispered, coming over to hug me.

"You heard I was here?" I groaned.

"Sure. Everybody in the shop has been talking about it. I guess they're coming from over here and spreading the word over there." She tucked my hair behind my ears, then held my face in her hands. "Poor thing. That must've been scary."

"You have no idea." For the first time since I'd found James Flynn, tears prickled behind my eyes. A delayed reaction, I guessed, brought on by stress and fatigue and being sad for a friend. I leaned in and let my big sister hug me.

And darn my weak soul, I wished I could call Landon. It was at times like this that a girl wanted to be able to go home to somebody who would understand and listen and love her.

"Maybe I should get a dog. Would you come with me to look for a dog?" I asked, my voice muffled against Darcy's shoulder.

"What?" she laughed gently. "Where did that come from?"

"I hate the thought of going home to an empty apartment," I confessed. "I just hate it."

"Honey, you could stay with me for a bit if you wanted to. You know the couch pulls out. I would love to have you."

I couldn't help but snicker. "What about the guy you're seeing who you didn't want to tell me about until you were sure it was worth the family meeting him?" When her face fell, I added, "Come on. You think I don't hear things? I'm not the only one whose personal business gets aired out around here."

"Mom…" Darcy grumbled, about to storm into the café before Mom came in and nearly crashed into her. I left them to it, deciding to show my face behind the counter for a while. Might as well set the story straight if I could.

And it didn't take long before I got the chance. Pierce Vaughan, Cape Hope's preeminent funeral home director and somewhat creepy guy—my opinion, though I suspected not many people would disagree with me if I dared voice it —approached the counter. "Emma. I heard about the unfortunate happenings last night." He adjusted his horn-rimmed glasses, grimacing.

"Yes, it was quite a shock. I just happened to be in the wrong place at the wrong time, I guess. Can I get you anything, Mr. Vaughan?"

"Is it true you saw the killing take place?" he whispered, his eyes larger than normal thanks to his thick lenses.

"No. That is patently untrue." I looked around the shop and realized the half-dozen customers present were listening. "I'll repeat myself. I didn't see what happened. I only tripped over the body after Mr. Flynn was already deceased. And I really shouldn't be talking about any of this, anyway. The police will do their job. I'm here to do mine. Now, Mr. Vaughan." I gave him my most sincere smile. "Is there anything I can get you from the case here? I just frosted the carrot cake squares a few minutes ago."

And darned if he didn't look disappointed. "Oh. I see. Ah, I already have my coffee over there." He pointed to his table before scurrying back to it. I gritted my teeth against a groan.

Fact was, Cape Hope was a wonderful place. I considered myself lucky to have grown up there and to have so many friends, not to mention more than a few aunties and uncles who weren't actually related but had known me my entire life.

This sort of nonsense, however, soured me. It was one thing to be aware of gossip but another to be the topic of said gossip.

And Mom didn't help. She came in from the kitchen, giving me a heavy dose of stink eye. "I told you not to tell your sister I told you about her beau," she hissed.

"Maybe if you had kept things private, like she asked, you wouldn't be hissing at me right now," I hissed back. "And I only brought him up because she asked if I wanted to stay with her for a while."

Mom blinked, totally innocent. "What does he have to do with you staying with Darcy?"

"Oh, Mom." I was barely able to keep a straight face. "Come on, now."

She finally got it—then swatted me with a dishtowel, scandalized beyond belief. "Emma Jane Harmon!"

"Took you long enough!" I laughed, ducking another swipe before I noticed a buzzing in my back pocket. "Truce, truce, my phone's ringing. It might be… important." I glanced around the room, choosing my words carefully before retreating to the relative privacy of the kitchen.

It was Deke, and I sure wished my stomach wouldn't give a funny little twitch as I answered. "Hi. I didn't expect to hear from you until tomorrow." Interesting. Knowing he was worth tens of millions colored my opinion of him.

Now, he wasn't just a rude jerkface with occasional thoughtful tendencies. He was a rich, rude jerkface with occasional thoughtful tendencies.

"I thought I would give you the chance to decide how you wanted to get together rather than waiting until tomorrow and putting you on the spot." Okay, so he was in a thoughtful mood.

"Tomorrow's Sunday," I murmured. "I normally help my mom around the café on Sundays, actually. But I don't want to wait, either. Do you think maybe you could come down here?"

And was I completely out of my mind? I had just gone through the wringer out there, and here I was, asking somebody else tangentially involved with the case to meet me and stir up even more gossip.

"I'd love to get an idea of where Chef Robert got his start." He chuckled.

Great. Now, if I went back on it, I'd look even more like the moron he already thought I was. Nothing mattered more just then than getting a look at his photos.

There had to be a way to get Robbie off the hook. Even if

it meant swallowing my pride and adding fuel to the gossip fire.

I swallowed back the lump in my throat, along with the feeling that this was a terrible idea. "Okay, great. Here's the address."

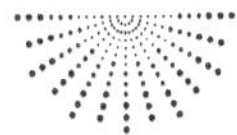

CHAPTER ELEVEN

I really did need a dog. Something to keep the apartment from feeling so lonely.

Now that the Righteous, Furious Rage phase had passed, I was sliding into the I'm Twenty-Six And Nobody Will Ever Love Me phase. The I Wasted Three Years Of My Life phase.

That, combined with the knowledge that a police detective with very pretty eyes and a square jaw had my name on a list of persons of interest, left me in need of a live-in friend. Somebody to comfort me as I binged ice cream and trashy TV.

Knowing I had work to do was enough to stave off the loneliness for a little bit. I pulled a half-empty bottle of Chablis from the fridge, poured a glass and called Marsha Wallis to explain what I could about the situation.

But she already knew. "Deke was in touch with me this morning," she explained. "To be honest, I was expecting to hear from you before now."

Yikes. Her voice was tight with what I could only

imagine was irritation. I hadn't expected that. "I'm sorry. It's been a wild day. I've never been through anything like it. I guess I don't have to tell you I'm innocent." At least, I hoped I didn't have to.

"I have no doubt," Marsha assured me. We'd never met in person, as her office was all the way out in Los Angeles, but I'd seen photos of her. An attractive, middle-aged woman, fit and healthy looking with a California tan. Probably surfed in her free time or something.

It occurred to me that I knew nothing about the way Californians lived.

"I'm just relieved the police let me come home, rather than keeping me in the area until they're finished with me. I don't know what else I could possibly provide. But I promise, I'm working on the article right now." Or I would be once I was off the phone.

"I'm glad to hear you don't intend to let this get in the way of your work," she replied, approval heavy in her tone.

"Not at all. A deadline is a deadline." And maybe I needed to stop using words that included "dead" since I was now shivering and remembering James's wide-open eyes.

"That's the problem, however, which I've been tossing around in my head all day," she confessed. "How to run this article while one of the main figures is now deceased, and the other is the prime suspect."

"Did Deke tell you that?" I gasped.

"Not in so many words, but I got the gist," she informed me. Terrific. One more person who assumed Robbie was guilty. I guessed I should be grateful she wasn't asking me to spin it with the murder in mind.

"So… you're saying you don't want to run the piece?"

"Perhaps not until this is put to rest. Right now, there are too many question marks in place. Is Chef Klein responsible? If not, who is?"

So much for my big chance at a new career. I flopped onto my sofa—careful not to spill wine from the glass in my hand because I wasn't that foolish—and sighed. "I see."

"That doesn't mean we don't want to run it at all," she was quick to point out, and I noticed her use of the word "we." This wasn't merely something she'd tossed around in her head. This was something she'd discussed with others.

"I understand," I fibbed. "What if Chef Klein is guilty?"

Her silence spoke volumes. "Is there another job I could take in the meantime?" I asked, hopeful.

"We have one in Miami you might be perfect for, actually!" Her relief was palpable.

Mine, however, was not. "Oh. I can't leave town for the time being. What with being a person of interest and all. I promised I wouldn't venture out of the state."

"Ahh. All right, then. I'll keep an eye out for local work you can do. In the meantime, by all means, get your thoughts about the food and the space down on paper before you forget them."

Yes, but that wouldn't pay, would it? I could just as easily write about it on my blog and at least make a little ad revenue. I was grateful to have kept the blog up and running, even if I'd planned upon landing this new job to back off from the work I did to keep the content fresh. I got plenty of organic search engine traffic without it.

Once my pointless phone call was finished and I felt lower than I had before reaching out, I looked across the living room to the kitchen. Except for the bedroom and of course the bathroom, the apartment was one open floor-plan. A countertop separated the kitchen area from the living area, and the dining area doubled as my workspace. It was lived-in, stuffed with houseplants and candles and framed photos.

And apart from me, it was empty.

I turned on the TV without caring what was actually on and went to the kitchen, pulling out my trusty mint-green stand mixer. "Come on, baby," I murmured, patting the sleek machine. "Let's make magic happen."

Baking was one thing which had always tethered me to myself, to what made me who I was. It was in my blood, something I'd learned to do before nearly anything else. I couldn't read yet, but I knew the ratio of ingredients for a solid buttercream frosting. I could temper eggs before I learned how to ride a bike, and understood why tempering was important.

Nobody wants scrambled eggs in their pastry cream.

I decided the bowl full of lemons on my counter was more than just a pretty display. They begged to be made into lemon bars. I got to work zesting, then juicing the lemons, before whipping up a shortbread crust in the stand mixer.

Was I kidding myself about being a writer? Maybe this was what I was meant to do all along. Blogging about food had at least allowed me to combine my two great loves. I pressed the crust into a rectangular pan and pricked it all over before sliding it into the oven.

I couldn't see working the way Mom did, however. The woman didn't have a minute to herself. And when she did, what did she do with it? Working on the books, settling the advertising budget, placing orders for more flour, sugar, eggs, coffee.

Because she loved it. I loved baking, but she loved the entire business.

Darcy loved what she did, too.

Heck. Even my father loved his job. Sometimes to the point of obsession.

When was I going to find something I loved? I thought I'd found it, but maybe this was a sign that I needed to look elsewhere. Maybe my entire life needed a shake-up, one much bigger than a new job.

The harsh buzzing of the doorbell made me jump and almost made me splash bubbling lemon curd all over myself. I took the pan off the heat before dashing to the intercom. "Yes?" I asked, leaning in. Sometimes people accidentally leaned on the bell while waiting in line to get pizza. The restaurant was that popular—I could hear voices downstairs as the place filled in on an early Saturday evening.

But it wasn't an accident. "Em? It's me. I heard what happened. Can I come up?"

My stomach turned to ice. Landon. The nerve of him. "Landon, I'm fine. I don't need comforting."

That was a lie. I did. I needed it badly. Nothing had gone right ever since we broke up.

But I didn't need him.

Even so, I knew he wouldn't leave well enough alone. I decided on a compromise. "Hang on a sec." I took the lemon bar crust out of the oven, turned the oven off, then went downstairs. He didn't deserve to come up. Not when he had defiled our life there.

He was waiting on the sidewalk, hands in his pockets, rocking back and forth from the balls of his feet to his heels like he always did when he was nervous. Good. Let him be nervous. Let him wonder if I was going to make a scene.

It was a good thing he had his back to me, because I was pretty sure my eyes got all big and misty when they first settled on him. No way could I let him see that. I allowed myself to remember those terrible, ugly moments when I walked in on him and Bimbette—I never did learn her name—and that wiped away any mistiness.

I then cleared my throat. He turned, and I was dismayed to find him as boyishly good-looking as ever. His sandy hair still flopped across his forehead, his cocoa eyes were just as deep-set and caring.

Not that I'd expected two weeks to change him that much, but it would've been nice if he'd grown warts all over his face or if his nose had fallen off.

"Hi." I folded my arms over my chest, glad I hadn't splashed any lemon curd or otherwise made a mess of myself. "Like I said, I'm okay. As you can see."

"You don't have to be so hostile. I wanted to make sure you're okay, not just physically. Otherwise."

I shrugged, forcing myself to remember every lurid, heartbreaking detail to keep from breaking down and doing something regrettable. "I'm in the middle of making lemon bars, so I guess I'm doing all right."

"Lemon bars." A smile played over his lips. "My favorite."

Of course. And I had subconsciously remembered that, hadn't I? And I'd decided to make them anyway.

"How did you find out what happened?" I asked, desperate to keep this meeting on-track.

He chuckled. "How does anybody find out anything around here? I heard it from somebody who heard it from somebody else. I heard you're a suspect."

"That's not true."

"I didn't think it was, but I thought you should know what people are saying."

"Very kind of you to keep me posted." If only you'd been so considerate when you started up with Bimbette.

"That must've been a horrible thing to come across," he murmured, brow furrowed.

"I've come across worse."

Zing! That got him. His face crumpled as much as a face could crumple. "Em," he breathed, crestfallen. Somehow, that was worse than anything else.

"Don't. Don't do that. Don't get all… that." I waved a hand around in the general direction of his face. "You don't get to do this. Thank you for checking in, but a text would've sufficed. I'm really okay. Thank you."

I turned on my heel, triumph surging through my veins. I got him. I got him! Granted, he set me up for it, but I took the shot and boy, was it worthwhile. I was even giggling to myself as I entered the apartment and locked the door before bursting out in full-strength, gut-busting laughter.

I got a little bit of my own back.

Little did I know how long it would be before I felt that way again.

CHAPTER TWELVE

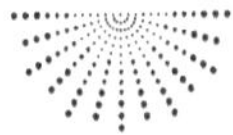

I wiped down the table near the window and used the proximity as an excuse to look up and down Main Street. It was a sunny day, the sort that turned my thoughts to summer.

Of course, in a shore town, summer was generally on everybody's mind most of the time. That was our bread and butter. At least, for the businesses closer to the beach. We were a few miles back and as such catered more to the people who lived in Cape Hope year-round.

Still, business always started picking up in mid-May. Mom was already preparing, as I knew from experience most of the businesses that made up the town's commercial district would be. Right down to the brand-new awnings, their vibrant colors a welcome change after a year's worth of sunshine had faded the last bunch.

"You'll rub a hole in that table if you don't stop wiping," Mom advised. At least she waited until she was by my side rather than calling it out across the café for everyone to hear. "Your gentleman friend will be here when he gets here."

"Mom. For the love of everything, don't call him that."

"Why not? Is he not a gentleman?"

"I wouldn't know either way. But it's the connotation I don't appreciate. He's a guy my editor threw at me, just like I'm the girl she threw at him. If it wasn't for the case, I'd be perfectly fine never seeing him again." I cornered her behind the counter. "And I would appreciate it if you would please, please not make any romance-centered remarks while he's here. I'll just die of embarrassment."

"The last thing I want to do is embarrass you," she cooed, stroking my hair.

The thing was, I believed her.

It was just that she had no idea how embarrassing she could be simply by being herself. I loved her dearly, with all my heart, but there was times when the woman went out of her way to embarrass me.

Like when she fanned herself upon Deke entering the café. "Is that him?" she asked, which of course meant every pair of eyes in the café turning his way.

He paused, looking around, looking slightly dazed at the silence which fell over the room. Yes, that was him. Yes, he looked good. It seemed button-downs tucked into well-worn jeans were his uniform, and I was okay with that. He made it work.

Rather than respond verbally to my mother, I chose to step out from behind the counter and greet Deke by the door. "Hi," I whispered. "And forgive her. She's... my mom, and she's great but... you know." There I went again, tripping over my tongue. It looked like the apple hadn't fallen far from the tree.

He grinned. "It's okay. This place is great, by the way. The whole street is so charming, for lack of a better word."

"It is, isn't it?" I glowed with pride. At least, it felt that way. Here, especially in the café, I was stronger. I felt like we were on even footing. "Have a seat. Can I get you a coffee? Something to eat?"

A few minutes later, I sat across from him with coffee and croissants between us. This was going to be great. I had everything under control.

"Would you like some coffee with your sugar?" he asked.

"Hmm?" I looked away from the stream of white granular heaven which poured into my coffee.

"Maybe some diabetes, instead?" Deke snickered. "I watched you pour those packets into your coffee at the station, too, and I thought for sure you were joking until you took a sip."

So much for thinking this was going to go smoothly. I placed the glass pourer on the table and picked up my spoon before very deliberately stirring the sugar into the drink. Never once did I break eye contact. "I like sugar."

"Evidently."

"I didn't think that was a crime."

"It isn't. Murder, on the other hand…"

"Lower your voice, please. We're in my mother's café, remember, and you know I didn't kill anybody."

He leaned closer, which was unfortunate since it meant smelling his spicy cologne. "I'm practically whispering, and nobody else besides your mother is under the age of eighty."

"Which means they wear hearing aids and can turn them

up real, real high," I informed him. "Trust me. They can hear everything."

"Sure can!" Mrs. Merriweather chimed in from clear across the room.

I grinned, wiggling my fingers in a wave, before turning to Deke with a flat expression. "The defense rests."

"Point taken," he whispered, glancing at Mrs. Merriweather and her yellow-veiled bluebird hat before looking back to me. "I guess sugar comes with the territory around here. Your mom being a baker and all."

I decided to let that slide rather than countering with the fact that he, too, was acquainted with the white stuff. After Raina's reveal of Deke's family history, I'd done a little digging. Mr. Bellingham's family was basically made of candy.

But for whatever reason, he chose to keep this quiet rather than speaking of his illustrious background. There had to be more to the story. I was willing to bide my time.

"I've basically been mainlining the stuff since I was in the uterus," I confirmed. "I was Mom's first taste tester. She didn't start the café until she was pregnant with me, and she had to test out her recipes, of course."

"Of course."

"If she ended up feeling wonky—nauseated and all that —she knew she had to move on to something else. If it stayed down and I seemed happy, she added it to the menu."

"Seems logical." He looked around. "I've gotta give credit where it's due. She opened a café while raising a family. I can't imagine how difficult it must have been."

"Neither can I. This was my daycare. I watched her work until she was almost ready to collapse some days, but I was too young to understand, you know? She still wakes up well before dawn and doesn't leave until closing time. My sister and I practically have to tie her down to get her to take the occasional day off."

"What about your father? How does he feel about not seeing his wife?"

I winced with a quick shake of my head. "Ix-nay on the ather-fay," I murmured through clenched teeth, looking to the counter. She was busy steaming milk for a latte, thank goodness.

"Oh." He grimaced. "Sorry. That was clumsy."

"Though maybe that answers your question, somewhat," I offered, looking down into my creamy, sweet coffee. Coffee loved me and made it possible to sit across from this man without starting an argument like I'd already become so good at. I took another sip.

"The café got in the way?"

"It's not like he wasn't married to his job, either," I made it a point to say, like I felt the need to defend my mother. Nearly five years had passed since the divorce, and I still felt the need to take sides. "Darcy and I always used to joke that we felt like the whole town was our brothers, sisters, aunts and uncles. Because he cared just as much about them as he did about us."

"But not all jokes are funny," Deke mused.

"Exactly. Sometimes we joke when we're trying to get a message through to somebody. He never got it. But he's happy now with his g-i-r-l-f-r-i-e-n-d." I spelled it out from behind my hand, just in case anybody was reading lips along with listening in.I then realized I'd spilled half my life story to this stranger to whom I didn't owe anything. "You're probably wondering why I can't stop talking," I offered before sipping my brew again for lack of anything else to do.

"I figured you're buzzing off all the sugar you're drinking. And the caffeine."

"What's it feel like, up there on your high horse? Ever get a nosebleed?" I took note of the way he drank his coffee. Black, no sugar. What kind of monster…?

"It's unhealthy, is all."

"Thanks for your learned medical advice, Doctor."

He rolled his eyes and obviously decided to let the matter drop, since he leaned in with his hands folded on the pink tabletop and generally looked like he was ready to get down to business.

"This probably isn't the best place to talk about this, now that I've found out how… curious the townspeople are," he whispered, "but I went through all the photos I took that night and studied them. I mean really studied them. And there's one point where James's demeanor changes visibly. It's like night and day. You remember how he was early on in the night."

"Sure. Mr. Personality. Big smile, a million teeth. Wants to sell you a used car."

He sputtered, choking a little on his coffee. I handed him a napkin. "Yeah. Something like that," he agreed when he'd gotten himself under control and his color came back to normal. "Then, after the toast Robbie gave, he changed. According to the timestamp, I don't have him in any pictures for twenty minutes after that. And when I do, it's like Jekyll and Hyde."

"*Jee-kill*," I corrected without thinking.

"Excuse me?"

"A common misconception. It's actually pronounced *Jee-kill*, not *Jeck-yl*."

He blinked. "And?"

"I don't know. It's just something I picked up. Anyway, go on." Me and my big mouth. Deke didn't seem like the type to discuss random literary trivia early on a Sunday morning.

"As I was saying," he continued with a little sigh, "something must have happened between the speech and the next time he showed himself."

"And the next time he showed himself, he must've been on his way out to the beach," I mused.

"Yes. There are no more pics of him after that. Except…" He looked down into his coffee, and I couldn't see his expression.

"Tell me you didn't take pictures of the body," I whispered. When he didn't, I wasn't sure if I admired him or what. "The police couldn't have been too happy when they found them."

"The police didn't find them."

I stood, holding onto the table for support. "I'm gonna get us to-go cups. We need to talk about this outside the café."

Yet before I had the chance, the door opened and revealed someone I would never have expected to see stepping foot inside that café ever again.

Once again, the room went silent.

This time, for my father.

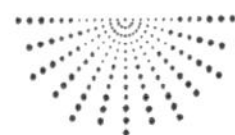

CHAPTER THIRTEEN

"Dad?" I asked, eyes darting back and forth between him and Mom. "What are you doing here?"

"You didn't answer your phone, and I needed to speak with you." He noticed Deke and gave him a brief nod. "Now."

Mom had gone stock still, the color draining from her face. I could only remember how much it hurt to see Landon again, how many mixed emotions had swirled around in my head and my heart.

That was after spending three years with the man. A far cry from the quarter-century of marriage she and my father had shared before everything fell apart.

I turned to him. "We should get out of here and talk someplace else. Next door." Darcy wasn't his biggest fan— she was Team Mom, all the way—but she wouldn't kick him out. Not if I begged her not to.

Deke followed us without asking if we wanted him to. I was starting to understand him a little better, and one thing had already become abundantly clear; he didn't hang much weight on social niceties. I made a mental note to revisit the secret pictures he'd hinted about.

Darcy's jaw fell when the three of us walked in with Dad in the lead. I threw her as apologetic a look as I could. But that wasn't enough. "What are you doing here?" she asked, coming out from behind the register to greet us. Or throw us out. I wasn't sure which way the wind would blow.

"We needed somewhere to talk that wasn't next door," I explained in a whisper. There were customers in there, even so early on a Sunday morning. And naturally, they all wanted to see how this would play out.

Darcy eyed Dad, which he pretended not to notice. One thing she and I had never agreed on and maybe never would was our view on how to treat him after the divorce. And his subsequent relationship with Holly, his girlfriend.

It was Holly who hurt Darcy worse than anything. She was barely ten years older than Darcy, twelve years older than me. Not young enough to be his daughter, but it still irked my sister something fierce that he had moved on with somebody who we could agree didn't hold a candle to Mom.

But that wasn't our business, not really. He was still our father, and it wasn't like he'd cheated on Mom.

"Don't raise your voices," she warned, arms folded over her chest like she was protecting herself. "And make it quick if you can."

I gave her another apologetic look before following Dad to the rear corner of the shop, between dusty stacks of secondhand books turned in for store credit. "What's this about?" I murmured, careful to look around for eavesdroppers.

He grimaced. "I wanted to give you a little more insight

on what I referred to yesterday. Before I drove away. Remember?"

My heart beat a little faster. "Sure." I looked up, over my shoulder, to find Deke standing just behind me. Strangely, his was a comforting presence. "He said there were lots of people who might have wanted Flynn killed."

"How do you know that?" Deke asked Dad.

Dad sighed.

"It's okay," I whispered. "You can say it in front of Deke. He's helping me."

"Helping you?" Deke asked.

If he only knew how to hold his tongue when it mattered.

"Helping you?" Dad repeated. "With what? When last I checked, I asked you to leave it to the police."

"And yet you took the chance of walking into the café, which tells me there was something you found important enough to step foot in there. What is it?"

"I only wanted to grant you a little consolation, since I know you're worried about your friend." He looked at Deke before continuing. "You know James Flynn owned property in Cape Hope. Up and down the coast, in fact, at times through shell companies and at times under his own name. We were already investigating after a handful of lawsuits were filed against him by vendors, contractors. There was quite a lot of questionable activity going on."

My palms tingled. My pulse raced. "So there were tons of people who might've wanted to kill him."

"But how many of them had access to the chef's knife?" Deke murmured, close to my ear. Like the devil on my shoulder. Just when I was starting to get excited.

I turned my head, looking at him. "Okay. Then I'll find out who did it."

"Emma. Don't make me regret sharing this information with you," Dad growled.

"I'm not asking you to tell me exactly who threatened to sue him, am I? No. You don't have to give me any specific information. Unless you want to," I added, hopeful.

"You know I won't."

"I wonder at Robert Klein getting himself mixed up with a guy like that," Deke mused. "I thought he was supposed to be smart."

"Yeah, but if he didn't know, he didn't know," I whispered with a dirty look.

"You don't have to get so defensive."

"I'm not!"

"Regardless," Dad interrupted, "that was what I had to tell you. Now that he's dead and word has spread down here, there's more interest than ever in learning who he screwed out of what. Pardon the expression."

"Could you tell me what you find?" I asked, hopeful again.

"What difference could it possibly make?" He wouldn't let me look away, holding my gaze. "Well? Tell me."

"I don't know," I admitted. "I have to do something, Dad. I have to feel like I'm helping. I can't let Robbie rot in prison when there might be a way to help."

He glanced at Deke, then sighed. "There is next to nothing you could truly do, you know."

"I'll be the judge of that." Deke snickered softly, but I pretended not to notice instead of stepping on his foot like I wanted to. I was proud of my maturity.

I knew my father's sighs. The one he let out then told me he knew when he was beaten—and that my sister was probably shooting us dirty looks from across the room, which meant time was growing short. "If anything comes up, I'll let you know. But."

I gulped. "But?" Of course, he wouldn't let me get off that easily.

"But I want a promise from you. Promise me you won't stick your nose in where it doesn't belong."

"Dad—"

"I mean it," he continued, his voice firm. "Stay out of this. Somebody killed that man. You don't think they would hurt you if they knew you were getting close to them?"

"He has a point," Deke murmured.

"Hush," I hissed.

"Maybe I should leave you in charge of her," Dad suggested, raising a brow.

"Oh? Like I'm a baby? Like I need to be babysat?"

He chuckled. "Emma. Promise me you'll be careful and stay out of trouble."

I crossed my fingers behind my back. "I promise."

Dad kissed the top of my head and slipped past me, making a quick exit. He looked to Darcy before stepping out, like he hoped she would turn toward him for once, rather than away, but he was disappointed. So was I.

Meanwhile, Deke touched the hand behind my back. "Your fingers are crossed," he observed with a wry laugh.

"Yeah? So?"

"So, I could've said something while your father was here but decided not to." He ran a hand over the spines of a row of books. "Because I respect you wanting to help a friend."

"Well, gee golly. I'm glad I've met with your approval." I tilted my head to the side. "What? Are you going to take my father up on it? Are you planning to babysit me?"

"Do you need babysitting? Are you going to keep behaving like a baby?"

"You literally just finished saying you respect me, and now you're calling me a baby. Which is it?"

"You tell me," he challenged. "Which do you intend to be? Somebody with guts, or a baby who whines?"

"You are so lucky my sister owns this store," I whispered, turning my back on him and working my way through the stacks to get to the door.

"Why?" he asked, and I hated the laughter in his voice.

"Because I might have pushed a pile of books on you." I waved to Darcy on the way out and noted her interest in Deke. I would have a few questions to field later.

"But then you would never get to see the pictures I took, would you?" he asked, patting the bag he still carried over one shoulder. I guessed his laptop was in there, and the memory card.

Upon stepping outside, I turned to him. Better to ask this question now, on the sidewalk, rather than wait to enter the café and run the risk of half the town hearing in time. "How did you take pictures the cops didn't see?"

He smiled, his eyes darting over my face. "I don't know if I'll tell you now. You threatened violence upon me."

"I'll do more than threaten if you don't tell me. Dad made sure I took self-defense classes for years. One of the benefits--or perils—of being a detective's daughter."

"But I don't intend to give you anything to defend your-self against, so I guess you won't have reason to put all that training to use."

Dang, he had an answer for everything. I could only shrug. "Please. Just tell me. I'll lose sleep if I don't know."

"Tell me the truth about something first, if you would."

"Can't you ever just give me a straight answer?"

"One question." He lowered his brow. "Just how close were you with Robert Klein? Or Robbie, as you keep calling him?"

I snorted before I could stop myself. "That's what you wanna know? What are you, jealous?"

"Curious." He didn't crack a smile.

What did I have to lose? "I had a crush on him when I was sixteen. We kissed one time, near the end of the summer. My first kiss. I call him First Kiss Robbie some-times. Do you want details, or is that enough humiliation?"

He pursed his lips. "First Kiss Robbie. Boy. You must really want to know about those pictures I took if you were willing to share that."

"You're right. I do. It was in the walk-in fridge, by the way."

"Okay, okay, forget I asked." He rubbed the back of his neck with a rueful grin. "You're tough."

"I know. Now. The pictures."

"Is there anyplace a little more private where we might look at them? I doubt the café is the best option, what with all the hearing aids set to top volume and everything."

"Good point. I'd say the library, but the head librarian is one of Mom's best friends and my godmother, on top of that. And she's also super into real-life murder mysteries.

She's thinking about starting a podcast and everything." I was rambling again and knew I was rambling again and needed to stop myself.

So what did I do? Simple. I came up with the worst idea I'd ever had. "Maybe my apartment?"

I went cold inside the second I said it. What was I thinking? Would he take it the wrong way?

Shoot. Had I left any underwear lying around?

"Okay," he agreed. "Lead the way."

Shoot. Shoot. Shoot.

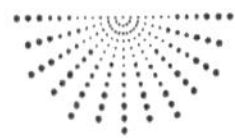

CHAPTER FOURTEEN

"You're sure your mom won't mind my stealing you away?" Deke cast an amused glance through the plate glass window, obviously noting the bustling crowd inside the café. And they certainly noticed him right back.

I had only gone in to get my purse and phone—sure enough, I had three missed calls from Dad—and was still psyching myself up for a trip to the apartment, where I hoped most fervently that I hadn't done anything to unwittingly humiliate myself before leaving that morning.

"I promised I wouldn't be gone for long," I explained. It was better not to mention the fact that my mother would in fact not mind him stealing me away at all. Granted, her idea of him stealing me away was a lot different than his idea.

She wouldn't mind if he swept me off my feet and carried me away into the sunset. Especially if she knew he came from a wealthy family, which at that point she did not. Because technically, I wasn't supposed to know, either.

I kept my inner thoughts to myself. "Besides," I continued as we started off down the street, "she has running the place down to a science. So long as I'm there first thing in the morning to help bake anything that needs baking, she's pretty much good after that. Sometimes, I think she would rather be on her own. Darcy and I only get in the way."

He chuckled, a wry grin lighting up his face. "I guess there's something to be said for autonomy, but not when it leaves a person unable to accept help."

"You're describing my mother to a T," I chuckled. "She's someone who would cut off her nose to spite her face when it comes to her business. Granted, she's a great person. Everybody loves her. I look up to her, the way anybody would. But she's just so darn stubborn."

"The apple most certainly did not fall far from the tree."

I rolled my eyes. "That is the second time you said something like that to me."

"You can't pretend you don't know how stubborn you are. I mean, honestly. Let's be serious. Your dad made a good point in the bookstore, you know. But I very much got the impression that you disregarded it the moment he was out of your presence, the way a stubborn person would."

"What point would that be?" There I was, thinking I could give him a tour of Main Street and regale him with stories of how I'd picked out my prom dress at the bridal shop across from the café, and how I'd once fallen and split my lip in front of the ice cream parlor down on the corner.

Granted, I would've left out the part where I'd cried more about dropping my ice cream than I had about any pain in my lip. Although knowing him, he probably would've inferred it without my saying a word.

"You know what point that would be. The point where

he asked you to keep your nose out of this investigation. He's right. Somebody out there was desperate enough to kill a man in cold blood. Anybody might've come by at any point that night. There were hundreds of people milling around inside the dining room, in the resort. That was a tremendous chance to take. What leads you to believe they wouldn't continue being just that desperate if they knew you were closing in on them?"

"I don't intend to be stupid enough to let them know I'm on to them," I grumbled. "What bothers me the most about this is the sense that the police went with the lowest common denominator when searching for this killer. Because you're right. It was a tremendous chance. And while there might have been hundreds of people there, how many people had access to the kitchen? So that rules out a great number of people. Of course, they're going to blame the person the knife belonged to, whose fingerprints were all over it and who'd just had an argument with James earlier in the evening. Why? Because it's easy, because it all fits on the surface. And because they don't know him."

"Neither do you." He eyed me warily. In fact, he might've taken a step further away from me after he said that, like he was waiting for me to lash out. Little did he know how wary I was to lash out in public, especially on a Sunday morning when it seemed like half the town was out taking their morning walk.

Most especially on such a gorgeous day. The air was so fresh, the breeze coming off the ocean and spreading the scent of salt over the town. No matter where I went in life, the smell of salt air would always mean home.

"I know he's a good person," I announced, and I meant it with all my heart.

"You said it yourself, you knew each other when you were sixteen. When was that? Ten years ago?"

"Pretty much," I admitted against my will.

"A great deal can change in ten years. Especially formative years like that particular decade. Be honest with yourself. You don't know who he changed into, or what he went through. I know he's traveled the world in his studies."

"Yes, I know that, too. He went to Paris, Naples. He studied in New York and LA. I know this."

"He's lived a lot of life. It's one thing to meet up with somebody after a decade and kiss each other on the cheek and compliment each other. It's another to really know someone."

I could hardly believe what I was hearing. I came to a stop at the corner, pretty much in the very spot where I'd had the unfortunate lip splitting incident, and turned to him. "Do you think he did it? Straight talk. Do you think it was him?"

"It doesn't matter what I think."

"Spoken like somebody who thinks he's guilty." I wished I didn't feel so disappointed. Since when did his opinion matter? He was probably one of the rudest people I'd ever known. Definitely not somebody whose opinion would matter under any other circumstances.

So why was I overcome with the desire to stomp my feet and pout? Why did his opinion make me feel so sad?

He shrugged. "I just think it would be best for us to keep an open mind. That's really all I'm concerned with. For us to keep an open mind in this."

I crossed the street, giving him no choice but to follow at a trot. "Okay. Let's say he did, even though I know he didn't. Let's just say for the sake of argument that he did." I stared straight ahead, rather than confessing how I used to dream of living in one of the sprawling, colorful gingerbread Victorians we passed. Homes with such grace, such grandeur, such history.

One of my favorite times of year was Christmas. For obvious reasons, of course, but especially because many of the historic homes were decorated inside and out in preparation for walking tours which always drew hundreds of people at a time.

Instead of sharing this—which I wanted to, for some reason—I felt the need to defend Robbie. "Why would he kill his business partner on the night of the opening? Why, when he put so much work into building this restaurant? The restaurant won't exist by itself, I imagine. It's attached to a hotel. James was the hotel part. Why would he jeopardize everything he'd worked for?"

"That's a good question. And definitely why I can't say for sure whether or not I think he did it. That's how you have to think about this," he reminded me. "Not with your emotions. With facts. The fact is, they had a lot riding on such a huge project, and obviously murdering his partner would put that in jeopardy. That's a lot easier for me to hang my hopes on than the fact that he was a good kid ten years ago."

"And a pretty good kisser, too." I glanced his way from the corner of my eye and noted his pained expression.

"It was your first kiss. How would you have known any better?"

"I've been kissed since then, thank you very much. I know what I'm talking about." This was devolving rapidly. "Okay. So he had too much riding on this to risk it all by killing James. Let's put him aside as a suspect. Who else should we be looking at? That sous chef. I would give my right arm for the chance to talk to him."

"I'm sure the police have already questioned him five ways from Sunday."

"That's great, but I haven't. And I was there in the kitchen. I saw how humiliated he was. James could really turn it on and off, you know? One of those people who could be just as sweet as pie on the surface, but who had a nasty streak a mile wide."

"We also know he was a scam artist, and maybe a thief."

"Fine. But again, what are the odds that one of his angry contractors or jilted business partners were present at the event?"

"You realize you're turning suspicion back toward Chef Robert, don't you?"

I was just opening my mouth to argue when a familiar voice called out across the street. "Yoo-hoo! Emma!"

I turned with a smile to find my Auntie Nell sweeping the sidewalk in front of the library. No matter how many times my mother reminded her that the town provided such services and her tax dollars paid for those services, Nell McGinty couldn't be persuaded to let anybody else take care of something she could just as easily do herself.

"Hi, good morning! That's such a pretty blouse!" And it was pretty, a fluffy pink blouse with puffy sleeves and a Peter Pan collar. She had long since chosen to ignore the adage that redheads weren't supposed to wear pink.

"Thank you! I've been meaning to check up on you after talking with your mom." Naturally, even though she spoke with me, her gaze kept drifting over to Deke. I could just imagine the questions she would pepper Mom with the minute she managed to get her alone.

Or, knowing the two of them, they wouldn't be alone. They would have an audience. An audience who would then take gossip home, or to their friends.

"Everything's fine, no worries! See you on Tuesday night?"

She nodded, giving a thumbs up before returning to her sweeping. Though I didn't know how productive she thought she'd be when she couldn't stop staring at Deke.

"And that was…?" he asked once we were on our way again.

I slapped my forehead. "I forgot to introduce you. Though I've never been one to enjoy shouting introductions across the street. That was my Auntie Nell. One of Mom's best friends, she runs the library. The one I told you wants to start her own true crime podcast."

He snorted. "That's pretty progressive for a lady of her age. And what about Tuesday night?"

"Is this an interview?" I teased. "Tuesday night's Book Club night. My sister picks the books, of course, since she always knows the best new releases. It's usually us and a few of the other ladies from town. Some of Darcy's regular customers, some of Nell's patrons."

Instead of smiling or at least patronizing me, I found him frowning.

I frowned back, shrugging. "What?"

"You're not going to be happy if I ask what I wanted to ask."

"You know I can't let you get away with that. Now I have to know what you had in mind."

"You asked for it." He drew a deep breath. "Do you have any friends your own age around here? It seems like everyone we met today is either related to you or roughly your mother's age—or older. What about young friends? Is there any sort of social scene around here?"

Why that made me so defensive, I didn't know. But then I hardly took the time to examine my feelings, either. "What are you trying to say? I didn't ask you to come down here to throw shade at my life. If you must know, I'll tell you the truth. But only because we're coming up to my apartment on the next block and I'd like to get this out of the way before we go back to talking over what's really important right now."

"Okay."

"Yes, there are young people around here. More once the summer tourists start coming in, but of course, they aren't the sort of people you become close friends with, if you know what I mean. They come and they go. But this isn't a party town, as you can see. In a lot of ways, it's sort of frozen in time. And a lot of the people who live here have lived here their entire lives, the way I have. They're my friends. I've known them since I was born. But it just so happens that right now, I'm also in sort of a transitional phase. The friends my age I've managed to maintain since moving back here after college are kind of in limbo right now."

"Limbo? Why?"

"Because I had a bad breakup recently, and I think everybody's maintaining their distance until things blow over. He still lives here in town, he moved in with his new girlfriend or whatever. At least they're on the other side of town, but still. Things are a little uncomfortable right now. My friends checked in on me, but they had their own lives to live, too. It's better for me to have a little time to breathe, some space and a chance to think."

"Now I feel like the world's biggest idiot for asking such a personal question."

We came to a stop in front of the pizza shop, and I turned to look up at him. Backlit by the sun, it looked like he had a halo around his head. I knew he was anything but an angel, but there was no ignoring the effect. "I agree. You are an idiot. But not the world's biggest. And now, you owe me one."

"I owe you one?"

"Yup. When I feel like it, I'm going to start asking questions about you. You already practically know my life story. But I don't know the first thing about yours." I turned to the door, pulling it open. "So brace yourself."

"Something tells me that spending time with you requires bracing oneself regardless." He chuckled, following me up the stairs.

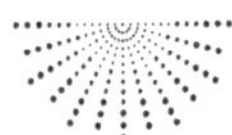

CHAPTER FIFTEEN

"Would you like some coffee? Since I didn't exactly give you the chance to finish what you had at the cafe?" As I spoke, I cast a nervous glance around the apartment. It didn't look like anything was too terribly out of place—not too embarrassing. If he'd been there a week earlier, he would've been in for a far different look into my life.

One involving pizza boxes and tissue boxes and even boxed wine. Lots of boxes.

"Yes, please." He set up his laptop on the dining room table. "This is a nice apartment."

"I love it. I really do. Even with the pizza shop downstairs. If anything, that's just convenient. I'm lucky he serves such a great slice."

"There's nothing like pizza from the shore," Deke agreed.

"Have you spent a lot of time at the shore, then?" Yes, it was time for me to learn little bit about him. He had already managed to interview the daylights out of me, and I had pretty much opened up the vaults and let my entire life history pour out.

"Around as much as anyone who grows up in this area."

"So you grew up around here?"

"Closer to New York. But of course, it wasn't summer without a trip to the shore."

"But the North Jersey shore is completely different than South Jersey. They're like two different worlds."

"Oh, so you're a shore snob?"

"Damn straight!"

He laughed. "Point taken. For what it's worth, I like the pizza better down here than I do up there. But I'm pretty sure I would have my New York credentials stripped if anybody found out about that, so that'll have to be a secret between the two of us."

I placed a cup of steaming coffee in front of him and winked. "Your secret is safe with me." What the heck was happening? Here I was, making jokes and being all relaxed and normal with this guy. It was like I had stepped into an alternate universe where things like this actually happened. Where people sat down on a Sunday morning over coffee and enjoyed each other's company.

That was something Landon and I hadn't done much of. He was always either working or watching TV or out with friends. And I was either cooking or taking pictures of my food or blogging or helping at the café.

I pushed those memories aside since they didn't matter anymore. What mattered was Robbie, proving him innocent. Now I felt like I had to prove myself to Deke, as well. I wanted him to know my instincts were on the money.

I pulled up a chair beside him as he opened the folder

containing his pictures. "Here," he offered, turning the laptop to face me. "I don't really need to look over them again. I spent a lot of time yesterday poring over them, from the first to the last."

I had to admit—if only to myself—that he knew how to set up a shot. His eye was impeccable.

"That's beautiful," I marveled at one of his photos, taken before anybody had entered the dining room. The last amber beams of light flooded through the windows surrounding the room, turning the white chairs and floor and walls to gold. It was absolutely breathtaking.

"Yes, sometimes Mother Nature decides to play along and drops a gift like that in your lap." I felt him looking at me, rather than at the screen. "But you would know that."

"What do you mean?" I asked as I went to the next picture, and the next.

"You've been doing your own food photography for years, haven't you?"

That stopped me cold. "How would you know that?" I asked, turning to him.

He shrugged. "What? You don't think I did a little digging? I wanted to know more about you, what qualified you to write that article."

Right. I should've known it would have something to do with him wondering if I was qualified. Not curiosity, not interest. His silly ego.

At least I knew there was nothing to be even the slightest bit ashamed of in the work I did on my blog. I might have started off small, not knowing what the heck I was doing, but my process had evolved over time.

"Well, now you know." I turned my attention back to the

screen, my tongue aching from all the biting I was doing. If I was going to prove Robbie's innocence, I'd probably need Deke's assistance. I couldn't risk turning him into an enemy now.

My nose wrinkled at the first sight of Aubrey in one of the pictures, but then I felt bad for it. Her husband was sitting in jail, most likely, and she had to be a wreck.

She wasn't a wreck that night, was she? Smiling brilliantly, friends with everybody. In that respect, she reminded me a lot of the late James Flynn.

Deke snorted, taking a sip of his coffee. "She was working the room, wasn't she?" he asked.

"Like it was her job. Hey, maybe it was. Maybe Robbie asked her to be his ambassador. I'm sure he had other things to worry about." She was another one I'd like to speak to if given the chance. She might be able to give me a little insight into the relationship between Robbie and James.

I kept this to myself, though. For some reason, I had this strange sense Deke would tattle on me to my father if he knew just how far I was willing to pursue this. A silly idea, since I was sure Deke didn't even know Dad's phone number. But I couldn't shake it, regardless.

I flipped through a few more photos. Nothing earth-shattering. There was one of me, and I remembered him taking it. I also remembered giving him a hard time about it. Now, all I did was cast a doleful look in his direction before moving on.

The first shot of James made me shiver. I couldn't help it. There he was, alive and well and vital and energetic. He had no idea that the moment that shot was taken, he had less than an hour left to live.

I got up, going to the window, rubbing my arms. "Wow. Sorry. I had no idea how that would affect me."

"And I admit, I didn't think of it, either. Maybe this wasn't such a good idea. And to be honest, I need to tell you this, but there isn't much here that would shed any light on the situation. Except for one section which I can skip to if you want."

I nodded, still looking out across the street. The storefronts were shuttered on a Sunday morning. I guessed there weren't many people in the market for stationary or knick-knacks or homemade candles at that time of day.

"Here we go." He was waiting for me, and wasn't this whole thing my idea? How would it look if I got all swoony and emotional when it was my idea for him to be there in the first place?

So I threw back my shoulders and returned to the dining room table, sitting next to him. Now that the initial shock had passed, I felt more at ease.

He'd clicked ahead to where Robbie and James gave their speeches. I could practically put myself right there in that moment. I was so proud of Robbie. And he looked so happy, didn't he?

Or did he?

"It's not easy, is it?" Deke asked, watching me as I went through the photos. "Looking at them, knowing what we know now. Wondering what might have really been going on under the surface."

"You're right," I admitted. That was exactly what I was doing. Now, I looked at the smiles with new eyes, and thought they looked a little tight. A little too strained. In one picture, Robbie was smiling in James's general direction, but his eyes were hard. There was no warmth in them.

I sat back in the chair, frustrated. "I don't know what I thought this was going to accomplish," I muttered, down-hearted. "What was I expecting? Something that would exonerate Robbie? Talk about naïve."

"Hey. I don't think you're naïve."

I burst out laughing. "Tell me another good one," I said with a roll of my eyes.

"There's nothing wrong with wanting to help a friend. But I honestly don't think there's much to be done here. There was bad blood between them, you can see it written all over their faces."

"But why? That's what I don't understand. That's what I want to know. Why did things turn around? They couldn't have started off badly, or else Robbie wouldn't have wanted to go into business with him."

"It's none of your business," he warned.

"It's not your business whether or not it's any of my business," I retorted, and I knew I sounded childish but what did it matter? "I appreciate you coming all this way to show me the pictures, but I think maybe it would be best for me to go my own way on this. You don't have to get involved."

"Maybe I want to see how this plays out," he suggested. "And maybe I feel, I don't know. A personal connection to the situation. After all, I was the second person to come across the body."

I eyed him with suspicion. "Don't tell me you're second-guessing whether or not I did it."

"Why would I do that? I mean, just because you were

crouching next to the body with your hand wrapped around the handle of the knife…"

"Oh my God, get out of my apartment if that's how you're going to be."

He laughed, shaking his head. "You are so touchy. I'm kidding. Still, maybe it bothers me a little bit to think of you doing this on your own. In spite of your father's warnings, and in spite of my warnings, I get the feeling you're not going to let this go."

"You're right." I shrugged. "I can't help it. I'd kind of like to know who did this. Maybe I can thank them personally for giving me the chance to stumble over a dead body and contaminate my first crime scene."

"Oh, I almost forgot. I was going to show you the pictures I took of the body."

I shivered again, like I had before. "I'm not sure I want to see it now," I confessed.

"Are you sure? Not even if there's something very interesting which I'm hoping the police figured out by now?"

How was I supposed to say no to that? He may as well have dangled a treat in front of a puppy's nose. Or sugar in front of mine. "Okay. What's up?"

"First off, look at James again." He found a photo of James giving his little speech, his glass raised in the air. With his arm lifted the way it was, his suit jacket had fallen open a little bit. Thanks to the angle Deke captured, a packet of papers was visible sticking out of the inside pocket of his jacket.

"Once I saw that," he explained, "I went back to some of the other pictures. You can see the outline of that packet over and over again. He must've been carrying those papers around all night."

"Interesting…" I looked at him, brows lifted. "What does it mean?"

He sighed, shaking his head. "I'm about to show you this, and you have to promise you won't tell anybody about it." To my surprise, he pulled his phone from his jeans pocket.

"You took pictures with your phone?" I asked, stunned. "What happens if they back up to the cloud?"

"They won't. I never let anything in my phone automatically back up, neither should you. Just one of those things I'm sort of passionate about." He opened a folder in his photo app and held the phone out to me. "Here. I don't know why instinct told me to take these on my phone, but that's what happened. I wasn't thinking clearly."

"That makes two of us. Remember, I touched the knife."

I took the phone, looking at the picture. There he was, just the way he was when I found him. Jacket hanging open, a patch of blood on his shirt with the knife in the center. "What am I supposed to be looking at?" I asked, my throat tight. It was grislier than I remembered, maybe because I'd been in shock at the time.

"What's missing?"

I looked again, and this time I saw what he was talking about. "His pocket is empty." Sure enough, there was nothing in that inside pocket.

"Not only that, but the lining is sticking out. See?" He pointed. "Somebody took those papers out of his pocket either before or after they stabbed him. They did it in a hurry."

"So I guess we can assume he wasn't the one who did it,

then. If he had taken the papers out of his own pocket, like in an office or something, he wouldn't have left the lining sticking out."

He nodded. "At least, I would assume not. Besides, from what I understand his office is at the top of the tower. He would never have the time to go upstairs, deposit the papers someplace, come downstairs and get himself murdered—as it is, not more than a few minutes at a time go by without another picture of him on here. Trust me, I checked."

"Whoever killed him wanted those papers." Our eyes met, and I was sure there were a million questions in mine.

"It would look that way." He said back in his chair, arms folded over his chest. "So. What do you think it means?"

I looked back down at the phone, then at the photo on the laptop. "I think it means I need to talk to that sous chef. And to Robbie's wife. Even to Robbie, if possible. Somebody's bound to know what those papers were about."

CHAPTER SIXTEEN

The resort sure didn't look the way it had on Friday. Amazing, the difference a weekend could make.

And a murder.

What was going to happen to it? Certainly, it would still open. Wouldn't it? All that work, all those jobs. It was in a state of limbo, what with both of its concerned parties out of commission for the time being.

The local paper sat beside me, on the passenger seat. The headline spoke volumes. LOCAL CHEF CHARGED WITH MURDER OF BUSINESS PARTNER.

And there was a photo of Robbie and James, the two of them smiling just minutes before the murder. That was the angle the press was taking. The fact that everything seemed just fine on the surface, that they had made toasts praising their partners just minutes before one of them plunged a knife into the chest of the other.

I was probably going to regret this. No, I was definitely going to regret it. But I had to try.

I continued, then, past the resort and deeper into town.

Paradise City couldn't have been more different from Cape Hope if it tried. The beachfront properties were all glitz and glamor, towering hotels and spas and the like, while further away from the shoreline was a different world of cinderblock apartment complexes and what used to be grand, Victorian hotels but had been converted to boarding houses.

The police station was around a mile from the beach. I parked in the lot and hurried down the sidewalk with my fingers crossed. Maybe the gods would smile on me and Detective Joe would be in a good mood today.

The gods were disinterested in my petty concerns, evidently.

"What are you doing here?" he asked when he saw me waiting at the desk. At least he'd changed his clothes since Saturday morning, now wearing a pale lilac shirt, purple tie and grey slacks. The man could coordinate.

I forced myself to stop taking mental inventory of his many delightful qualities in favor of looking him in the eye. Gosh, they were still the same pretty shade of jade. "Uh. Um." What was I doing there, again?

"Well?" He did not look amused, swishing a plastic stirrer around in his coffee. "Out with it. Did you remember something you couldn't recall this weekend? Maybe some-thing to exonerate your old friend?"

That made my cheeks burn. "You don't have to be nasty," I whispered, careful not to make a scene in a bustling station. "But of course, this is in relation to Robbie being charged."

"Of course," he echoed, looking me up and down. "I have

the feeling I'll regret this, but come on. My office is this way."

His office. I had stepped up in the world. He led the way, not bothering to take it slow for my sake, and I tripped over my feet as I tried to keep up. It seemed I had trouble with my coordination lately. Though at least it wasn't a dead body tripping me up this time.

His office was more like a cubby, but that didn't surprise me. In fact, it brought Dad's office to mind. Shelves stuffed to overflowing, the desk piled high with folders. Maybe five empty coffee cups.

And in the wastebasket, a pile of chewed-up coffee stirrers. Maybe Joe wasn't the cool cookie he pretended to be. Maybe he took his stress out on strips of plastic, chewing them to pieces.

He closed the door. "What brings you here? Let me warn you, I have a ton of work to process."

"I understand. I only wanted to know if you found the papers missing from James Flynn's suit jacket."

That surprised him. How could I tell? Easy. He dropped into his chair like his legs had given out on him. "What papers?" he asked in a way-too-casual tone.

"The papers that were in his jacket pocket throughout the night. I've seen pictures from earlier in the evening and you can see a folded packet in there. There was no such packet when I found him."

"And how do you know that? Were you looking for them when you found his body?"

It was time to lie like a rug. "Do you remember the first body you ever saw? The first dead one? I do, and it was James Flynn, and I can't forget a single detail. His jacket was hanging open. I would've seen white papers against a dark blue lining. They weren't there. I close my eyes, and I see him. But I don't see the papers."

Maybe it was a detective thing, the ability to hold a person's gaze so they couldn't look away no matter how much they wanted to. All this time, I thought it was just my dad.

Joe stared at me, immobile except for the twitching of a muscle in his jaw. "Do you play poker?" he asked out of nowhere.

"Not generally."

"Good. Because you'd lose your shirt."

"Are you saying I'm lying?"

"No. I'm saying you're lying, and you're terrible at it."

I dug my nails into my palm. It was one thing to threaten to knock a stack of books onto Deke's head, but I couldn't go around threatening a police detective. "The papers weren't there. Did you find them? That's all I wanna know."

"It isn't any of your concern." Then, he smirked, leaning across the desk. "Or is it? Maybe you knew what was in those papers."

"Huh?" I leaned back, away from him.

"Yeah. Maybe you knew, and you took them after finding the body."

"No!"

"Maybe you knew they had something to do with your old friend, so you took them out of his pocket."

"Why would I go out of my way to ask you about them, then?"

"To throw me off." He shrugged, sitting back, stirring his coffee. I wondered if he wanted to chew on the stirrer. I wondered if my presence was the only thing keeping him from doing it. "What do you think? I think my theory sounds solid."

"I think you don't know what you're talking about, with all due respect."

"With all due respect, I think maybe you knew there was bad blood brewing between the chef and his business partner, and you let the memory of teenage love muddy your thinking. You heard them arguing and you decided to take matters into your own hands."

"If that's really what you thought, why did you charge Robbie with the crime?"

"Are you trying to talk yourself into a trip to jail?"

"No. Of course not. But one, it wasn't teenage love." I held up one finger, then added another. "Two, I knew nothing about the relationship between Robert and James until I overheard their fight."

"Eavesdropped on their fight?"

"Happened to be in the same room as they were in while they were fighting," I concluded, glaring at him. He seemed to accept this. Or, at least, he didn't have a comeback for it. "Anyway, I knew nothing of any bad blood. People argue. You're the one telling me there was bad blood, not the other way around."

His face went blank for a second. Then, to my surprise, he chuckled. "You got me there," he admitted, spreading his hands in a gesture of surrender. "I said too much. You have a way of getting me talking, Miss Harmon."

"Please. Emma. I haven't been called Miss Harmon since grade school, and that was usually when the nuns were annoyed with me."

"I can't imagine why anyone would ever be annoyed with you." Before I had the chance to say something that might get me into trouble—it was hard to remember he was a cop, not somebody I could mouth off to with impunity—he leaned in again.

This time, he didn't look so tough or sarcastic. His mask slipped, as it were, and it revealed a decent guy trying to get through a difficult case. Just like on Saturday, I noticed how tired he looked. Even his voice was softer when he spoke again.

"Look. Emma. I understand you're concerned about your friend. I do, really. And no, I don't personally think you killed James Flynn to protect your friend. Though I have to warn you, and I shouldn't be saying this, there have been others who've suggested it."

"Others?" I squeaked.

"Don't worry," he was quick to add. "I don't take them seriously. It isn't my first case. I've been doing this for ten years." Funny. He looked no older than thirty. I guessed keeping in shape had its benefits, and I instantly began questioning my sugar addiction.

Still, the thought that someone might've fingered me for the crime left me cold inside. Who would do such a thing? Heck, nobody at the event knew me besides Robbie. And I doubted he would accuse me.

"Who was it?" I had to ask.

"I can't tell you."

"That's not fair. You shouldn't have said anything if you weren't going to tell me who it is."

"You're right, I shouldn't have said anything. I wish I hadn't. But no, the specific information shared during interrogations cannot be revealed." He shook his head, sighing. "You have to learn to leave well enough alone."

Yet another thing the nuns had tried to drill into my head. It hadn't worked then, either.

"Can you at least tell me if you knew about the papers that are missing? Did you even pick up on that? I know you have all of Deke's photos."

"Ah. The two of you have been talking this over."

"We were working together. We're still working together, technically, although the article we were there for has been postponed since, you know. There's this whole unfortunate murder thing going on."

"Yes, it is rather unfortunate." I thought he might have been trying to hide a smile. "Well, I'm sorry about that. But just because you're cooling your jets right now doesn't mean you should turn your energy toward trying to solve this case. I would appreciate if you would leave it up to me."

"How am I supposed to leave it up to you when you have the wrong man sitting in jail?"

"Did it ever occur to you that there's evidence you're unaware of? That maybe, just maybe, you don't know every-thing about this?" Just like that, he went back to being the guy he'd been before. Brusque, difficult. He stood, going to the door, opening it without much flourish. "And as I've said many times already, I'm very busy. I've given you all the time I can spare."

"You have the wrong man," I whispered, rising. "I'm sure of it."

"Thank you for your expert opinion, but it's time for you to go. And by the way, I was under the impression that you're staying in Cape Hope, under your father's supervision. Stay away from Paradise City unless I ask you to come in for more questions."

Oh, my cheeks burned with the heat of a million suns. And the thing about me was, I tended to cry when I was really and truly angry. That futile sort of anger, anger that couldn't be expressed without dreadful repercussions. Having to hold it in was the worst, having nothing to do with all that furious energy.

Since I couldn't scream it out, it tended to come out in the form of tears. Hot, stinging, frustrated, humiliated tears.

They prickled behind my eyes, threatening to make themselves known. I barely managed to blink them back as I summoned every ounce of dignity I could gather. "I haven't needed my father's supervision in a long time," I informed him in an icy tone. "I don't appreciate you making me out to be a child. I'm a grown woman. I don't need anyone to supervise me."

His face fell just a tad, and his mouth opened like he was about to apologize or at least admit he'd misspoken. But I was not about to give him the opportunity, since there was a good chance I was about to burst into tears and didn't want to further humiliate myself.

Instead, I turned on my heel and practically ran to the door, then flew down the stairs. It wasn't until I reached the sidewalk that I even drew a breath, and when I did, it was shaky. Ragged.

What was I thinking, coming here? I should've known someone as stubborn and pigheaded as Detective Joe Sullivan wasn't about to listen to anything I had to say. Would it kill the man take me seriously? I had real insight into the supposed killer, and he treated me like I was nobody. Like a baby who needed Daddy's supervision.

I drew a few deep breaths, welcoming the fresh air into my lungs. It was so stuffy and dry in that station. No wonder everybody was in a bad mood.

There was a park across the street from the station, and the squealing of children caught my attention. Kids never failed to turn my mood around, and this was no exception. I crossed the street rather than heading back to my car, knowing if I didn't find a way to release my anger I would only stew the entire way home.

Encased in canvas sneakers, my feet slapped the sidewalk. It was going to be a warm day, so I removed my cardigan and knotted it around my waist. There was something satisfying about the feel of sun on my bare arms and shoulders. Maybe I would finally get a little color after a long winter.

I smiled at the kids on the swing set begging the grownups to push them higher and higher. I used to be that way, too. I always wanted to see if I could touch the sky. Or at least go all the way around the top bar.

If I'd ever gone all the way around the top bar, I probably would've let go of the seat in utter shock and that would've been the end of that. No more swing sets for Emma.

It was a flash of auburn hair which first caught my attention. The sort of shade that tended to draw the eye, especially in the sun. I looked at the person that hair belonged to and something snapped into place.

He was the sous chef. I recognized not only his hair, but the wooden gauges in his earlobes and the tattoo on the nape of his neck. He walked with his head down, hands in the pockets of his khaki shorts, in a hurry to get somewhere.

I was after him before I knew what I was doing. "Excuse me!" I called out as I jogged behind him. "Excuse me, haven't I seen you before?"

CHAPTER SEVENTEEN

"Rob's a good guy." Kyle Norris sat across from me on the threadbare sofa, dead in the center with his arms stretched out to either side. They were long enough—or the sofa was small enough—that he nearly spanned the entire length from fingertip to fingertip.

"I agree. I'm devastated by this, honestly. Have you known him long?"

"A few years." He was very vague, this sous chef of Robbie's. Kind enough to invite me over to talk about the case, but otherwise not forthcoming.

He lived in one of the apartment complexes I'd taken note of on the way to the police station. A long, squat building. Brown brick. Inside, the apartment was small but serviceable, with the sort of furniture that told me it had come with the place. Undistinguished, old, very much used.

But it was clean, and I got the impression the young man sitting in front of me had struggled even to get this far.

"Did you study formally?" I asked. "I know Robbie— sorry, Rob, it's a bad habit—studied all over, but some restaurant workers learn in the kitchen. Hands-on. Which were you?"

"Hands-on," he grinned. "I started as a dishwasher when I was in high school and worked my way up."

"That's really cool. My mom has a café—that's how I know Rob, of course—and I know how hard that alone was. I can't imagine working in an actual full restaurant."

"It's not easy," he admitted. "But it's probably the only thing that's ever made sense to me, you know? School and all that?" He waved a dismissive hand.

"It's not for everybody," I allowed.

"Yeah, well, I wish somebody had told me that years ago. I could work myself to death in school and not get anywhere. It never made any sense to me. Or I could work myself to death in a kitchen and actually earn a living and have a decent life. I was never gonna go to college or anything like that. It's not me. But then I got in trouble, like, five years ago. I met Rob after I got out, and he offered me a job working under him once he got his own place." He sighed. "Look how that turned out."

I couldn't get a feel for the guy. He seemed sincere enough, but was he? What had he done time for? It was none of my business. Besides, plenty of people learned their lesson after going to jail and they didn't deserve to be punished for the rest of their lives. That didn't make him a killer.

Though it did make me wonder if I should maybe have learned a little bit about this guy before I accepted his invitation to visit his apartment. Alone.

"I'm sure that once they find who really did this, Rob will be free and the restaurant can open."

He leaned forward, elbows on his knees. He couldn't seem to keep his hands still. They kept moving, fingers flexing, fists tightening and loosening. I couldn't take my eyes off them. Was it a violent crime he had been locked up for? Those hands could easily strangle a person.

"Yeah, but what about the resort? I talked to some of the people who had jobs there. Housekeeping, you know. They haven't heard anything. It's like everything just stopped. Even once it opens, if it opens, is anybody gonna want to come?"

"For one thing, I think they will. People are morbid."

He laughed. "That's true. I already had a few people who knew I was gonna start working at the restaurant stop me and ask if I saw the body or what."

"I guess things aren't so different here than they are in Cape Hope." I smirked. "I can't tell you how many people have already stopped me, thanks to my mom telling them I found James Flynn's body. I sort of want to tell them to get lives, you know?"

"Yeah, I know." He looked at me, sizing me up.

He was decent looking, I guessed, if a little rough around the edges. He had been clean-shaven on Friday, but now sported uneven stubble along his cheeks and chin. He needed a haircut, his auburn locks curling over his ears and neck.

As usual, it was the eyes that drew me in, and his were dark and hard. He was a guy who had seen things in his life, unpleasant things. I had to bite my tongue to keep from blurting out the question at the forefront of my mind. Why was he in jail?

And I guessed Joe and his team must've known Kyle had

spent time in jail. He had to have a record somewhere. With that in mind, in as sympathetic a tone as I could muster, I asked, "Have they brought you in for questioning? I was in twice."

He frowned deeply, throwing himself back against the couch cushions, staring at the scarred coffee table. "Yeah. I was in there talking with that Joe What's-His-Name. Not my favorite guy. Kind of a dick."

"Believe me, I agree with you there. So he gave you a hard time, too?"

"He had me there for three hours that first night. Three straight hours. I didn't know which way was up. I'd been working all week straight, prepping for the opening. Both me and Rob were half out of our minds, exhausted. We were excited, too, you know? There was something to work toward. I thought I was on my way to Easy Street."

"How so?"

He shrugged, looking around at the beige walls, devoid of decoration. "What you do think? With a steady job, decent pay—Rob was really generous, he wanted to make sure his staff was taken care of—I could leave this place and move into a decent apartment. Someplace nicer. Maybe even rent a little house, who knows? I was really looking forward to it."

And I was sure his story could be repeated word for word by countless people. Whoever had plunged the knife into James's chest may as well have plunged it into the chest of every other person contracted to work at the resort. "That's terrible. I'm sorry. But I'm sure it's only temporary."

"Yeah, but if they don't find out who really did it, and if somebody doesn't step up and take charge of the resort, what are they gonna do? They'll probably have to sell it, I guess, and it'll take forever to change hands and all that."

"Hmm. Good point." I was starting to wonder if I had the wrong person in mind for the murder. Here was a guy who had a lot to lose. Every employee had a lot riding on this. Granted, maybe not everybody had thought things through beforehand, especially if they had enough of a problem with James.

That was why crimes of passion were called crimes of passion. They weren't crimes of thoughtfulness.

"I have a confession to make," I murmured, placing the iced tea which Kyle had so generously provided on a coaster. I had to give it to him, he did his best to keep the place tidy. Most men living on their own wouldn't be that way. "I was in the kitchen when James tore into you and the rest of the staff on Friday night."

Instantly, his face changed. His brows drew together, his nostrils flared. "Oh, really? Is that what this is all about?"

"No! No, not at all. I just want to tell you that I felt bad for you that night, that's all. It seemed like he had a really bad temper. I kept trying to tell Joe about it, but he didn't seem to take it very seriously. He only cared that Rob and James had a little argument afterward. I don't blame Rob at all, I would've told him to mind his own business, too."

"That was one thing they butted heads about a lot. James couldn't stay out of Rob's business. He didn't know the first thing about running a kitchen. It was obvious. Rob was the expert, and he tried to be nice about it first. He really did. I guess after a while, everybody eventually reaches the breaking point. He finally had enough of it."

I didn't know if he was referring to the argument or if he

actually believed his boss—somebody willing to take a chance on him and give him a second start in life—was a cold-blooded killer. Or maybe I was sitting in front of the killer right now at this very moment and he was trying to mislead me.

Maybe I should've listened to my father when he told me to stay out of it.

I cleared my throat. "Was he like that with everybody? I mean, verbally abusive and stuff?"

Kyle winced, his shoulders lifting. "I don't know. I heard rumors. Like he was a tough guy to work for. I heard from a few people who used to work at one of his places that they would sometimes not get their checks until two, maybe three weeks later. James would always swear would it never happen again, he always had an excuse."

"But I bet it did happen again," I mused.

"Yeah, I bet it did. There were a couple of times I walked in and found him meeting with some pretty rough looking characters. Guys who looked like they were pretty ticked off, to put it mildly. But he smooth talked them, just like he always did. He could smooth talk his way out of anything. But I got the idea that Rob was tired of being sweet talked. They started snapping at each other in front of us, the staff."

"That's never a good sign," I agreed. Meanwhile, the picture he was painting for me was simultaneously becoming clearer and more muddied with each word he spoke. Maybe I needed to call my father and ask exactly the sort of people James Flynn was involved with. I even considered asking Joe, but I knew he would just laugh in my face and tell me to get a life.

He bit down on his lip, like he was trying to decide if he

should speak his mind. "To be honest with you, I sort of got the idea that—"

I was holding my breath, waiting for him to reveal the idea he was sort of starting to get, when his front door opened and a woman's voice called out. "They didn't have the ice cream you like, babe, so I got another brand. I hope that's okay."

It was then that she turned after locking the door behind her. And I was pretty sure she was close to dropping the paper bag of groceries when she found company in the living room.

If I'd been holding something, I would've dropped it for sure. Because the woman standing in front of me was none other than Aubrey Klein.

And she had definitely called Kyle *babe*.

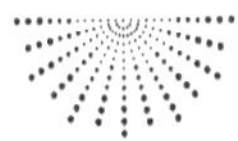

CHAPTER EIGHTEEN

"Aubrey, this is Emma Harmon." Kyle stood, taking the bag from Aubrey's arms.

My cheeks were burning. I could only imagine my face looked about as red as a beet. "I'm sorry, I didn't mean to, you know…"

Aubrey glared at me. "What? You didn't mean to what?"

Boy, she was just as friendly now as she'd been on Friday night. Then again, if my husband was currently in jail for murder, I would probably not be the nicest person. "It's just that had I known you would be here at any point, I wouldn't intrude." This was easily the most uncomfortable I'd been all day, which was saying something.

Meanwhile, as I scrambled for an explanation and an apology, about a million voices screamed different things in my head. All of them had to do with the fact that, oh my gosh, Aubrey was having an affair with Kyle. I was looking motive straight in the face. What better motive was there than for a jealous lover to kill his boss's business partner and frame the boss?

I could just imagine it all in that very instant. Befriending Robbie, earning his trust, getting a job from him as a ploy to spend more time with Aubrey.

Then, framing him for murder.

Suddenly, Aubrey's hostile expression softened. "Wait a second. Oh, no." She burst out laughing, covering her mouth with one hand. I didn't get the joke.

When she had herself under control, she managed to sputter, "He's my brother! Kyle is my brother. What, did you think? He was my boyfriend?" She giggled helplessly, leaning against the wall next to the door. She hadn't taken so much as a single step forward since she first came in and found me.

Now that she mentioned it, they did look a lot alike. Their hair, for one, roughly the same shade of red though hers was brighter. The same dark eyes, the same creamy complexion and finely chiseled features.

Though Aubrey had certainly taken better care of herself than her brother had. He was a lot older around the eyes, and he had the slightly yellowed teeth of a smoker. She didn't. In fact, she looked like she might've had her teeth whitened at some point in the recent past. Maybe in preparation for the opening.

"Oh! Okay." I laughed, too, only mine was the laughter of relief. It was like a release valve, letting out all the tension. "Sorry. I got the wrong idea."

Aubrey finally sat on the sofa, crossing her slim legs and wedging her purse between herself and the arm. Even in casual clothes, the sort of thing a girl wore when she went to the supermarket, she looked like a million bucks.

Some people were just like that. Raina was another one.

Even her so-called lazy clothes were name brand, well-fitted, hand wash only. She tried.

"We weren't really introduced on Friday," I pointed out. "Robbie—"

"I know who you are. I know my husband once worked for your mother. He told me all about it after spotting you at the opening."

If it weren't for the iciness in her tone, I might have been flattered. Granted, I'd never been married. Maybe a wife didn't like her husband bringing up an old acquaintance with another woman.

I decided to chalk this up to overwrought nerves. If I were in her position, I would've been a mess. Surrounded by balled-up tissues, empty wine bottles and ice cream containers, in the same clothes I'd worn for three days. When I considered this, Aubrey looked even better in comparison. Even her hair was immaculate.

I took another tack, wondering how to get through to her. I might not get another chance like this. "I just want to say I'm so sorry for all this. Honestly, if there's anything I can do, I'm here."

She nodded, her lips pressed together in a thin smile. "And exactly why are you here?" she asked, eyes narrowing. "I heard you're a writer. Do you plan on writing about this?"

Geez, no wonder she was so cold.

"No! No, not at all. It seems like we keep misunderstanding each other. I came to town today to ask the detective how things were going and why he charged Robbie with the killing. It's obvious to me that he doesn't have a murderous bone in his body. Of course, he acts like I don't know what I'm talking about and dismisses maybe three-quarters of what I say."

She jiggled her foot from side to side the way Raina did when she was annoyed, her thin smile returning. "Yes, he has that way about him, doesn't he?"

"Please, don't tell me he gave you an attitude. Of all the people he should be nice to right now, you should be at the top of the list." This was true, but I had to butter her up a little, too. Get her to like me. Even if I wasn't writing about the case, she had no reason to trust a word I said. How to get her to open up?

She shrugged thin shoulders which, when she raised her arms to pull back her long hair, flexed with hidden strength. One of those women who actually took the time to care for her body. I appreciated that, even if I never could find the time or willpower to attend regular yoga or Pilates classes.

"I guess when you're in that position and you see as many violent crimes as he probably has in a place like this, you lose a bit of your humanity. Your sense of empathy." So she clearly wasn't a fan of Paradise City. I made a mental note of that.

"How is Rob? Have you seen him?" I tried not to sound too over interested or concerned while making a point of not calling him Robbie. No sense giving her the wrong idea. She seemed the jealous type.

Lines appeared over the bridge of her nose as she winced. "About like you'd expect. Upset, confused. Natu-rally, he had nothing to do with this. The evidence is circumstantial, at best. Sure, they had their differences. All business partners do. If anything, I would think it's some-thing like a marriage. Occasionally, there's a blowup, but things calm down and smooth over and everything is all right. I suppose the detective wouldn't understand anything about that, so he thinks a few little arguments are enough to drive a person to murder. It's ridiculous." She rubbed her arms briskly as if it were cold in the room.

"You said a few little arguments? Kyle said something about that, too. James wasn't easy to be around, but he had a temper."

She rolled her eyes. "Oh, if you only knew. In the last month or so, my husband began questioning whether he'd made the right decision in aligning himself with James Flynn."

Even as my pulse picked up at hearing something new, my heart sank a little further. It seemed like everything I found out made Robbie's position more difficult. "How so? If you don't mind my asking, that is. And like I said, I don't intend to write about this. I'm here as a concerned friend."

She shrugged this off. Maybe it just didn't matter anymore. "He was never very forthcoming with me, you have to understand that. He would hint things here and there. My husband is a very private person when it comes to matters of business. Maybe he thought he could shield me from it or something, I don't know. You know how men can be sometimes."

"Yeah, I know that. I know what it's like when you're with a man who keeps things from you."

"Right? Like they think you can't be trusted with the truth. Frankly, I would very much have liked to know what his problem was with James, since my life is affected by his choices, too. Sure, it's his business, but it's our life. Our livelihood. If there was something I needed to know, I wish he would've told me."

I nodded, clicking my tongue in genuine sympathy. "I'm sure that was really hard. Honestly, my dad was like that with my mom. He's a detective. And he never wanted to tell her what was going on at work because he didn't want to burden her with it. Except she ended up feeling isolated. And he felt isolated, too, because he was deliberately holding back from her instead of sharing."

She snorted like she understood all too well. "How did they get past that?"

Maybe this wasn't the best example. "They didn't. But that doesn't mean you guys won't. I'm sure that once all of this has blown over, you guys will have a second chance to make things right. I'm sure he wants nothing more than to be with you again."

She chuckled. "I think first, he would open his restaurant. That's all he's cared about since he and James decided to go into this together. I mean, literally. He has lived, breathed, existed simply to open this restaurant."

"It was his dream," I murmured, heartsick. And somebody had taken it from him. I refused to believe he was the one who killed James, just like I couldn't believe Kyle would do it. Both of them had way too much to lose.

She raised her hand to her forehead, trembling. Her eyes filled with tears. "I just don't understand who would do this. After all that work! All the sacrifice. All the time we didn't spend together, all of it in service of something bigger. His dream. We put our lives on hold for his dream. And somebody took it away. I only wish those stupid detectives would get their heads screwed on straight! I know he couldn't have done this!"

She then burst into tears, covering her face with both hands, rocking back and forth. I went to her, patting her shoulder.

Kyle joined us a moment later, sitting next to his sister and pulling her into his arms. "It's gonna be okay. It's all gonna be okay."

I wanted to believe it. I wanted everybody to have a happy ending. I only wished it were possible.

This case was more complex than I could've imagined at first. If James did business with the sketchy characters Kyle described, it could've been anybody. Where to begin when the list of potential suspects was a mile long?

Aubrey continued weeping and it didn't look like she was about to calm down any time soon. I'd overstayed my welcome.

I patted her shoulder again and gave Kyle a sympathetic look. "I should go. Thank you for taking the time to talk to me, I really appreciate it. Please, feel free to give me a call. And please, I beg you, let Robbie know I'm thinking about him. I'm doing everything I can to help him. I won't let the police steamroll him, even if it means asking my dad for help."

I couldn't help but laugh at myself a little. After all, what was I supposed to do? I couldn't even figure out who had a motive strong enough to be worth murdering the man. There just had to be a way, was all.

I left the apartment feeling lower than I had when I left the police station. It seemed like no matter how high I climbed, I ended up slipping right back down to where I started. As soon as something made sense, something else came in and mixed things up again.

"Find anything interesting?"

I jumped out of my skin at the sound, then the sight, of Joe Sullivan waiting for me outside the apartment building. He leaned against the railing leading down to the sidewalk. Hands in his pockets, ankles crossed. The picture of ease on a sunny, spring day.

I knew better. There was tension in every line of his body. He was a coiled spring ready to pop. He would end up popping at me.

"I can explain—"

He held up his hands, and I tried not to fixate on his muscular forearms now that his sleeves were rolled partway up. *Not the time, Emma, not the time.*

"I don't remember suggesting I was interested in your explanations." He removed his sunglasses, his eyes narrowed and fixed on me in a steady, disapproving stare. "You have no business being here, and that's a fact."

"He was walking in the park across the street from the police station! What, was I supposed to pretend I didn't recognize him?"

"Yes. That's exactly what you were supposed to do." He sighed heavily, propping the glasses on top of his head. "Did you know he was Robert Klein's brother-in-law before you came here?"

"No. I only found out when Mrs. Klein arrived."

He nodded. "Yeah, it seems like she helps him out. You know, making sure he stays on the straight and narrow." That would explain the tidy apartment, I guessed. She came around regularly.

"Really, I had no idea. I only wanted to talk to him after I saw him walking through the park." Then, something occurred to me, and I became the injured party in a flash. "Did you follow me?"

"Me?" He placed a hand over his chest, gasping like he was surprised. "Why would I ever do that?"

"You did. You were following me!"

"If you must know, Miss Harmon, I followed you at first because I wanted to apologize for upsetting you. You ran out before I had a chance. By the time I stepped outside, you were already halfway across the street. I watched you catch up with Kyle."

"Do you think he did it?"

"You know I won't answer that question. Why do you bother asking?" He replaced his sunglasses, fixing them over his face. Really, they did him no favors since they covered his eyes. Easily his most striking feature, which was saying something since he was pretty striking all the way around.

I followed him to his car. "Seriously! Do you think he had it in him to do that? What was he in jail for?"

"You're crossing the line, Emma."

"Oh, come on. At least tell me I wasn't totally asking for trouble by going into the apartment of an ex-con."

He burst out laughing. "Ex-con. There's that Criminal Justice minor."

Once again, I had to remind myself that threatening an officer with bodily harm was probably a crime. "Please, just tell me if I should be careful about speaking to him again. You know, whether I should be alone with him or not."

"That seems fairly simple to me." He opened the car door, leaning on it before he slid inside. "Just don't see him again. Problem solved. That way, it won't matter what he did to land himself in jail."

I fell back a step, crushed. "Did you ever have one of those dreams where you're late for school or work or whatever, and it seems like no matter how hard you try there's no getting out the door? Like everything's deliberately standing in your way?"

His mouth pursed. "I guess everybody has."

"That's how I feel right now. I'm fighting as hard as I can to prove Robbie didn't do this, that he's not capable of it. I've always had a thing about being able to read people. You probably think it's dumb, but it's true. My dad always wanted me to become a cop, to follow in his footsteps, because he said I had excellent instincts. Sure, he's my dad and he's supposed to say nice things about me, whatever. And sure, it blindsided me when I walked in on my boyfriend and another woman, but—"

"Huh?"

Maybe he didn't need to know about that. "Never mind. My point is, except for that, I'm good at reading people. I've always been good at it. Robbie is a sweet, kind soul. Genuine. Not fake and plastic like James. I knew that much right off the bat. And he wanted that restaurant so badly. It was his lifelong dream. He never would've jeopardized it, and he wouldn't have committed murder right outside of it, for heaven's sake!"

He was going to tell me I was spinning fairytales out of thin air, wasn't he? That I needed to go back to writing about food and keep my nose out of serious matters. I braced myself for it.

"No. You don't have to be worried about anything from

Kyle," he muttered before sighing like a man with the weight of the world on his shoulders. "He was a dumb kid who got mixed up with the wrong people. That's it. Okay? You feel better?"

To a degree, especially since Joe didn't shoot me down.

Though I couldn't deny that it would've been easier to find out Kyle was a violent criminal capable of murder. "I guess?" I shrugged. "Maybe?"

"Unfortunately, Emma Harmon, that's as good as it gets with a case like this. Very rarely is there a satisfying conclusion. I wish there was, sincerely. With a detective father, you must know how frustrating it is when the case won't settle itself the way a cop wishes it would."

"Do you wish it would settle itself one way or another?" I couldn't help asking.

There was a beat before he chuckled. That beat could've held a great many thoughts and wishes. "Stay in Cape Hope, Emma. For your safety, if nothing else."

"Do you think I'm in danger?" I asked as he got into his car.

"All I'm saying is, you're running around asking a lot of questions and so sure I arrested the wrong man." He looked up at me before closing the door. "If you're right, there's a killer out here somewhere."

He left me standing there, speechless, as he drove off.

The jerk didn't even offer me a ride to the station to pick up my car.

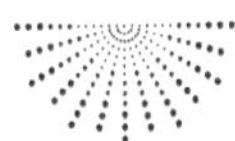

CHAPTER NINETEEN

On a good week, I wondered why we bothered holding Cape Hope Book Club meetings.

Even when it seemed like most of the attendees had read the book—or at least the first few chapters before skipping to the end—the conversation usually devolved into topics completely unrelated to anything literary within the first thirty minutes or so.

Once the wine started flowing, all bets were off.

And that was on a good week.

This week? After news of the murder had spread? The murder of somebody who owned property in Cape Hope? To say nothing of the fact that it had been I who'd discovered his body?

This was not a good week. This was maybe the worst week.

It was also the most packed my mom's house had ever been for this particular event.

"Standing room only," Darcy murmured on her way past with a pitcher of sangria.

I was carrying a platter of cheese and crackers which I placed beside a platter of fruit, nuts and honey. Many of those in attendance—twenty-two at last count—had brought treats with them.

Probably to make up for the fact that they hadn't read the book. How did I know? Because I had never seen them at a book club meeting before.

That and the fact that they followed my every move like I was the dot at the end of a laser beam and they were a bunch of cats. I wanted to turn around and demand they stop staring, but that would come off as too wacky even for this bunch.

And they were wacky. Most of them were friends with my Auntie Nell, who was probably the one who'd spread the word about the meeting in the first place. The house was packed with her library pals who happened to share an affinity for murder.

I was somewhat on the morbid side, but I had nothing on her crew.

She helped Mom carry in a tiered tray of fresh cupcakes, which took a place of honor in the center of the dining room table. "Well," Mom breathed, beaming. "I have to admit, I never expected this sort of turnout."

Her voice was just as sweet as could be, the way it normally sounded. Rarely had she ever raised it that I was aware of, not even the time Darcy and I got into a buttercream fight in the café's kitchen.

But that didn't mean she couldn't shoot her best friend a dirty look. So she knew this was all Nell's doing. I wondered if Raina and I would be like those two when we got older.

I couldn't imagine my impossibly chic best friend dressing like a holdover from a Southern gothic novel, however, so that was out. Nell made a big to-do out of fluffing the ruffled lace cuffs of her gauzy white blouse, seemingly oblivious to my mother's ire.

"I suppose we should begin," Mom suggested with a sigh. "Did you all bring your copies of the book?"

I had mine. So did my sister, seated beside me at the head of the table. All the better to get the first crack at the food, which was one of the main reasons I attended these meetings at all. Sure, I liked to read, but we hardly ever discussed the book anyway.

A few of the others, the regulars, held up their copies. The rest did not, looking guilty and shifty as they exchanged glances.

My poor mom. She had no idea what to do.

I stood, wishing I'd taken a fortifying sip of sangria before now. "Okay. I think we can all drop the pretense of being here for Book Club when most of you aren't actually in the club. At least you brought snacks, which is really nice. I can't wait to tear into that olive tapenade, whoever brought it. Anyway, you want to talk about the murder. I get it. Do you have questions for me?"

Mom let out a sigh and sat down, fanning herself with a napkin. "Thank goodness. I didn't know what to do."

"It's okay. I've got this." I looked out over a sea of faces. Some familiar, some not so familiar. Most of the women attached to those faces had their hands raised. Sheesh. I chose one at random.

She cleared her throat. "Nina George, I work at the library." Several of the women murmured in response and I wondered how I'd ended up in Bizarro World when all I wanted was sangria, snacks and a couple of hours of girl time. "What was it like? Did you touch the body?"

"I didn't. Except for tripping over his leg, which I guess doesn't count." I looked down at my sister, wondering if I was hallucinating this or if she was witnessing it along with me. Her half-hidden grin told me it was the latter.

I recognized Breanna Schultz from yoga class, back when I used to go to yoga class. "Was there a lot of blood?" she asked, eager.

"No. I mean, it was dark, but I don't think so."

Several of the women whispered to each other, and I had to wonder what I'd said to make them disapprove. I thought I heard one of them claiming she would've seen whether there was blood, dark or not.

I was halfway ready to tell her I wished it had been her instead of me, but I was in my mom's house and she was actually there and everything. My poor tongue would never recover from all the biting I'd done lately.

"Who's that cutie you were sporting around town a couple of days ago?" somebody asked from the back of the living room before I called on her.

Mom fielded that one for me, bless her heart. "I told you, Frankie. That's her gentleman friend."

Darcy pressed a freshly-filled wine glass into my hand.

"He's not..." I took a deep, calming breath that didn't actually calm me, but it was better than screaming. "He happened to be taking pictures for the article I was supposed to be writing about the restaurant opening. He was the second person to see the body. He was nice enough to drive in to show me some of the work he did that night."

"I wouldn't mind him showing me some of his work!" Mrs. Merriweather chirped from the easy chair, causing no end of knowing laughter.

I drained half the wine in my glass in a single gulp.

"Okay, ladies," Mom called out, holding her hands above her head. "Emma's love life is not the subject of this meeting."

"He's not even—" I started, then realized I was fighting a losing battle. Like trying to fill a bucket when half the bottom had fallen out. "Anyway. Let's move on. What else do you wanna know?"

By the time an hour had passed, my voice was about to go and I felt like a wrung-out washcloth. I had nothing left to give, plus my sister had been feeding me sangria throughout the process so I was a little unsteady. Mom announced it was time to eat and socialize.

I wondered what we had been doing until then and why it wasn't considered socializing.

I was glad to turn to the food, since I needed something to soak up all the wine in my otherwise empty belly.

Breanna-from-yoga caught up to me, tugging my sleeve. "Hey. I just wanted to say I'm sorry this is all happening. It really sucks."

My voice was barely a whisper, and not because I was trying to be discreet. "Yeah, it does."

She twirled the end of her long braid, chewing her lip as she continued hounding me. "I shouldn't have asked the question about the blood, but it just seems strange to me that there wasn't a lot of it. My mom's a nurse, and the first thing she said when she heard of this case is that there should've been a ton of blood if he was stabbed in the chest. I mean, it should've gotten everywhere."

"The knife was still in his chest when I found him," I explained, still whispering, before popping a tapenade-covered cracker in my mouth. If I had to live on one thing and sugar was off the table, appetizers would be my next choice. I could make entire meals out of them.

"I know, but still. Unless a person knew just where to insert the knife, it would be a bloodbath. You have to get pretty close to somebody to plunge a knife into their chest. Something would be bound to end up on the person who did it."

"Hmm. You're right, I guess. I never thought about it that way."

"And there wasn't a lot on him, either?" she asked, stroking her chin.

The girl had my attention. Maybe this night wasn't a complete loss. "No. A small pool on his chest. That's it."

"Hmm. Maybe whoever did it knew where to stab to kill him right away. Otherwise, it seems like a pretty big coincidence that they happened to do it where they'd cause the least about of blood loss and kill him quick enough that he didn't try to pull the knife out."

This girl was straight-up blowing my mind, and not because I was leaning toward tipsy thanks to my sister's bartending skill. "That's true. I mean, if there was a knife sticking out of your chest, wouldn't you try to pull it out?"

"Exactly. So they hit him right where they needed to on the first blow. That's pretty lucky for them, I guess."

"And for him, I guess," I added. "Less suffering."

"What if he was drugged?"

He had been drinking an awful lot of champagne that night. And alcohol was a blood thinner. But there had hardly been any blood at all.

Maybe somebody had drugged one of those glasses of champagne before he took it.

Maybe he'd gone outside to clear his head, wondering why he was suddenly so woozy.

Maybe that same somebody had followed him, knowing he'd be woozy and knowing he wouldn't fight back.

I left my plate on the table and took her by the arms. "Breanna, you're a very interesting person and I'm sorry we haven't spent more time together. That might have to change. Excuse me, I need to make a phone call." I elbowed my way out of the house and onto the wraparound front porch on which I'd spent so many hours dreaming as a kid.

Never did I imagine calling a detective about a murder I'd stumbled into.

"Sullivan." That was how he answered. His last name. Nothing more.

"Detective Joe?" I asked, pacing the length of the porch.

He paused. "I said it was me. Who is this? Who's calling me Detective Joe?"

"Emma Harmon."

"Why did I not know that before I asked?" he sighed. "Only you would call after nine o'clock."

"Oh. It's that late? Why are you still at work?"

"Because I find it so gosh-darned fun. Why are you calling? Are you in trouble?"

"Unless you count a book club meeting that turned into me being grilled for an hour by curious and well-meaning neighbors as being in trouble, I'm okay."

"I don't know. That sounds like trouble to me. What's the matter?"

"Did the toxicology report come back yet? On James Flynn?"

"What?" he spat. "Why are you asking me about this?"

"Somebody gave me an idea just now. What if he was drugged in advance of the killing? It makes sense, right? I mean, whoever did this had to get the stabbing just right. It couldn't be a quick crime of passion sort of thing, done in anger. Not when they struck him in exactly the right place on the first try. He must've been slow, woozy. Maybe he had already fallen on the ground!" My voice was getting louder all the time, even though it had practically left me during my impromptu talk.

"Emma—"

"Either way, it was premeditated. It had to be. Nobody gets that lucky without advance planning. Somebody drugged him."

He paused for one long, silent beat. "Are you drunk?"

"No!"

"Have you been drinking?"

"...no?"

"Jesus."

"What does that have to do with anything? Everybody knows Book Club is code for drinking wine and gossiping. Big deal. That shouldn't negate what I'm telling you."

He sighed. He was very good at sighing. "Maybe you'll listen to me now, while you're under the influence, since you sure don't listen while you're sober. Stay. Out. Of. This. Investigation. Do you realize you're wasting my time right now? I could be doing something worthwhile, but instead,

I'm listening to inebriated ramblings from a would-be super sleuth."

That hurt. I couldn't deny it. "Silly me, thinking somebody would be interested in learning the truth."

"Now, wait a minute."

"I mean, you have a man in jail when he stood to lose his shirt—his entire wardrobe—if this project went under. He had more to lose than just about anybody else. Meanwhile, it looks more and more like this was a premeditated crime, meaning that Robbie wouldn't have done it even in a fit of rage. Who stabs once, then leaves their fingerprint-covered knife behind? It just doesn't fit together."

He waited. When I offered nothing more, he asked, "Is that it? Or are you planning to tell me more about how I ought to do my job? Since you're such a hit at book club meetings, maybe I could have you come in and lecture the force on proper detective work."

"Forget it," I snapped, then ended the call before he could keep being mean. I wanted to throw the phone for good measure, but that wouldn't be any help.

Instead, I made another call. "Deke? I want to see your pictures again. This time, I know what to look for."

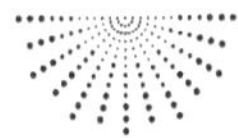

CHAPTER TWENTY

"Remind me what we're doing here?" Raina asked from the passenger seat as we cruised down darkened streets, looking for a garage with reasonable parking rates.

"We're lurking around to see if we can get into the resort even though it's not technically open yet," I explained. "Twenty dollars? Why would I spend twenty dollars to park? Jeez!"

"If you don't pick a garage soon and get it over with, you'll end up spending more than that to refill your tank," she pointed out. Always reasonable, my best friend. "Could we just park someplace close to the resort, please? I don't love the idea of walking around here at night."

She had a point. Beyond the beachfront businesses, the town wasn't exactly friendly to a pair of young women walking together in the dark.

"I don't know how I let you talk me into things like this," she whispered just loud enough for me to hear, looking out the window.

"I heard that."

"I wanted you to hear it." She giggled, taking the sting out of her words. "Honestly, this is one of your worst schemes. We're never going to get close enough to see anything. They probably have everything locked up. And if they're smart, they have somebody guarding the place. Probably a few somebodies. I'd bet anything."

"Sure, they do. And we'll be quick about it. I just want to see inside the restaurant and get an idea of how much time actually passed between my leaving the kitchen and going outside. I want to time myself walking around the pool."

"Why? I asked you why over the phone and you wouldn't tell me then."

"But you drove down, anyway. Which tells me you must think I have the right idea."

"Or I'm concerned about you sneaking around in the dark, alone," she countered. "Em, I know how much this means to you, and I want to help you, but I can't encourage you to take risks. And this is risky."

"Why? It's the beach. No big deal."

"The beach at night. In the dark. And this isn't Cape Hope. You don't know people here. Gosh, back there you can't swing a dead cat without hitting at least three people who've known you since the day you were born. But not every place is like that."

"You're so worldly," I teased, trying to lighten the mood.

"I'm trying to be serious."

"So am I. You know I wouldn't keep pressing on this if I didn't think I was on to something. If I thought there was even a slight chance of Robbie committing murder, I'd shake my head and click my tongue and move on with my life. I'd be sad, sure, and I would probably devour every word written about the case. But I'm completely positive he could never have done this, and I can't sit back and let the wrong man rot in prison if he's convicted. I feel it in my gut."

I knew from the sound of her heavy, put-upon sigh that she was about to say something I wouldn't like. "Are you sure you're not looking for something to take your mind off the break-up? It's okay if you are!"

"Wow, Raina."

"I'm sorry. I'm just trying to be your friend. I'm not trying to hurt you. If anything, I'm trying to keep you from being hurt."

"There's no chance of being hurt by anybody but my best friend, who thinks I'm enough of a loser that I would do this as a means of distraction."

"I didn't call you a loser, and I never would! You know I wouldn't. You know I love you. But it's because I love you that I feel I should say something, that's all."

"I appreciate it, but it's unnecessary. I know what I'm doing. Somebody has to speak up on Robbie's behalf. Somebody has to care about him enough to go the extra mile, because nobody else has but me."

"You don't think Detective Hottie McHotterson is doing his job?"

I snickered. "I can only assume you mean Joe."

"Oh, so we're on first name basis now?" Raina was good at that. She could change the subject easier than most people could change a lightbulb.

"Sorry. Detective Sullivan."

She waved a playful finger. "No. You can't take it back. You already called him Joe. So you don't think he's doing a good enough job? No wonder he gives you a hard time when you call him. I don't think I would like it very much, either, if somebody kept second-guessing my work."

"I'm only trying to help." I finally settled on a garage which charged a *mere* fifteen dollars for the first hour and pulled into the first empty spot I found.

"Sure, but did you ever have somebody hover over your shoulder when they were only trying to help? And you knew you had things under control, and you didn't really need them to help, but they insisted on hovering anyway? How did that make you feel?"

I hated when she made a good point like that. Maybe I closed my car door a little louder than I needed to before replying, "Like they thought I was incompetent. Like they were trying to tell me they didn't trust me or believe in me."

She wrapped a knee-length cardigan around her slim frame, nodding as we walked out of the garage. Her look this evening reminded me of Audrey Hepburn, ballet flats, fitted slacks, a white button-down. Even her sneaking-around clothes were more stylish than mine.

"Exactly. My point is, he must feel the same way. No wonder he's so brusque and abrupt with you. I would be the same way, quite frankly. And I know you would too, because I've seen how it irks you when people look over your shoulder when you're working."

"Okay, I'll grant you that. But this isn't like a group project in school where one person thinks they can tell everybody else what to do. This is life or death stuff."

"I'm with you all the way. Whatever you decide to do. You know that." She linked an arm through mine as we walked toward the beach. "I just don't want you to get in trouble or get yourself hurt. I can't help it."

"I'm doing my best."

"I also don't wanna see your butt get thrown in jail for sticking your nose in police business and insulting a cop."

I scoffed with much more confidence than I felt. "Can they do that? I don't think they can do that."

"You would know better than me. I bet if you got him mad enough, he could charge you with tampering or something like that."

She was right. He probably could. Which made this little adventure that much less exciting, while making not getting caught that much more crucial.

Okay. Maybe it was still exciting.

"When did you say Deke will be available to meet with you again?" Raina asked.

I noticed her head swinging back and forth, like she was scanning the area around us for shady characters.

"Not until some point this weekend. He's photographing an event in Miami that I could be writing about right now as we speak if I was allowed to fly there."

"I think that's ridiculous! You should've asked your dad to talk sense to Detective Hottie."

"I don't need my dad to fight my battles," I muttered. "Besides, I don't know… Besides." I pretended not to notice her soft sigh of disagreement.

The resort sat like a tall, dark guardian at the end of the beach. So much promise in that unlit sign, the out-of-place palms swaying slightly in the sea breeze. It was enough to break my heart when I thought of all the work Robbie had put into making his restaurant something special.

"It could be so good," I whispered, my throat tight. "The food was outstanding. I've been doing my absolute best for days to polish up my thoughts on it so when the article finally gets published, he'll get the kudos he deserves."

"And he will." She touched her head to my shoulder. "You have the best heart of anybody. Sometimes I forget to tell you."

I only gave her a playful nudge, because what could I say to that?

The closer we came to the building, however, clearing the dunes which blocked our view of the first few floors, the lights which burned inside were evident. "That's more than just a few guards," Raina observed. "What's going on?"

"Beats me." Darn, I wished my pulse didn't pick up speed at this turn of events. I had never considered myself the Nancy Drew type before now, but it seemed like I had a thing for mystery. A latent affinity for solving the unsolvable. At least, that was how I thought of myself as we approached the building.

It was more exciting than thinking of myself as a snoop who couldn't leave well enough alone.

"I don't know about this; people will see us," Raina whispered, like there was anybody nearby to hear us. But it didn't stop her from bending over the way I did, creeping over the grounds.

"It'll be fine. Now I wanna know what those people are doing in there. Are they getting ready to open?" I hoped so, I truly did. It would mean the business might start making money, that Robbie and Aubrey wouldn't go bankrupt while he awaited trial. Kyle and all the other staff members could start working, too.

I was glad I'd chosen to wear dark clothes, the two of us crouching behind a row of potted plants just yards from the inside of the restaurant. The kitchen lights were on, as were the lights over the bar, but nobody was visible.

Yet.

"Shh!" I hissed even though Raina wasn't saying a word, as Kyle emerged from the kitchen with a bottle of what looked like beer in one hand. There were a couple of strangers behind him, taking notes as he pointed here and there, talking a mile a minute. "That's Kyle, the sous chef. Aubrey's brother."

"What's he doing?" Raina breathed next to my ear.

"I have no idea," I breathed back. But he looked a lot more take-charge than he had back at his apartment earlier in the week. The word that came to mind as I watched him strutting around was *peacock*.

"He's walking around like he owns the place," she whispered, reading my mind. "Are they opening without First Kiss Robbie?"

"I guess they have to. Maybe he's giving those people Robbie's orders, you know? They worked very closely together on the project, Kyle said so."

"He would know better than anybody what Robbie had in mind, then," she mused. "I wish we could hear what was happening in there."

"Maybe you should go in and ask."

Both Raina and I gasped before falling on our butts at a man's voice behind us.

I scrambled to my hands and knees and looked up, panic-stricken.

Then groaned when I recognized none other than Joe Sullivan, aka Detective Hottie McHotterson, glaring down at me.

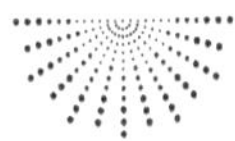

CHAPTER TWENTY-ONE

"We weren't trespassing. This is outrageous." Raina tapped her foot on the patio, arms folded. "We were only…"

Joe's brows lifted. "Yes? You were only what?"

"Looking around," I finished. "We were only looking around."

Joe slowly turned to me, unblinking. The man was flat-out unnerving. "Looking around at what?" he asked, his words clipped and precise. "What could you possibly be looking around for in the dark, when there is nothing to see out here but a covered pool and empty lounge chairs?"

"I only wanted to get an idea for how long I was out here exactly before I stumbled over James's body. That's all. That's literally the only reason we were here. I wanted to be precise. I thought maybe I could pace around the patio the way I did that night, try to remember the things I thought about and how long I thought about them."

I folded my hands in front of my chest like I was praying. "I'm serious. You have to believe me, please."

He snorted, his mouth a thin line of disapproval. "It didn't look like you were pacing the patio when I found you. You were squatting behind these plants like Lucy and Ethel, only not half as funny."

"You need to update your TV references," Raina whispered.

"I'll pretend I didn't hear that." Joe snickered, surprisingly good-humored. Maybe he liked Raina better than he liked me. "You know what I mean. What were you doing when I found you? You weren't walking around."

"Well, I couldn't very well pace around the patio while Kyle and those other people are in there. I didn't expect anybody to be inside except for maybe a few guards."

"Guards who would have considered you trespassers and probably would've called the police had they discovered you. Did you ever think about that? Do you ever think at all?"

"Do you always need to get personal?"

He scowled, dropping the amused act. "I take it personally that you don't think I can do my job, Miss Harmon."

I didn't dare glance Raina's way since I knew she would have a smug look on her face after predicting exactly how Joe felt. "I only wanted to give you the most precise information I could. That's it. Anything to help Robbie."

"Yes, well, there are plenty of people who want to help Chef Klein. Including his wife and his brother-in-law."

"What do you mean?" Raina asked.

"Chef Klein signed power of attorney privileges over to his wife earlier today, and she's now moving forward with the opening of the restaurant. Since the partnership between the two men included a clause granting full rights to the surviving partner should something befall the other, Aubrey Klein is now single-handedly in charge of opening and maintaining the resort. She plans to do so within the coming week."

I needed to sit down. There was a low, stone wall edging the patio on two sides, and it was lucky that I happened to be standing near it. I sank onto the cold, hard stone, shaking my head. "I guess that's a good thing."

Joe burst out laughing. "Yes, that's a very good thing. There are hundreds of people whose livelihoods depend upon this resort opening. Not to mention Mrs. Klein, and the chef. He'll need the money for legal fees, at the very least."

"Maybe you can finally get your article published!" Raina's voice was filled with hope and relief.

Yes. I might be able to do that now that the restaurant would be opening, even if it opened without Robbie being present.

I just wished I could feel better about the whole thing. Something didn't sit right with me, leaving a pit in my stomach. I looked up at Joe, only to find him staring down at me. "Well? Right now, this is as good as things can be. Considering that I haven't arrested you for trespassing, your night is looking better all the time."

"I wonder why they had that clause in their agreement," I murmured. "Doesn't that seem strange to you? I mean, I'm no legal brain, but I wonder which of them came up with that idea."

"When will you learn to leave well enough alone?" Joe scowled, glancing at Raina. "Is she always this impossible?"

"Only when an old friend is in jail for murder." No

matter how hot she thought he was—and he was hot, no doubt about it—Raina was not about to take any such talk from anybody. Not when it was me being talked about that way.

Joe turned to me again. "You're right. It is strange that clause like that was in their agreement. Especially considering that James ended up dead. I wonder, if I did a little digging, whether I would find it was Robert's idea to include it. Wouldn't that be something?"

That was the thing. That was what bothered me most. Knowing how bad it looked for Robbie that the two men had already agreed to transfer ownership of the business to the other should an accident or some other tragedy befall them.

It was enough to make me wonder about James's other business partners. Whether they had the same sort of clauses in their contracts, or if this was unique to Robbie and him.

I thought I knew who I could go to if I really wanted to find out.

"Well, okay. I guess that settles that." I sprang to my feet, taking Raina by the wrist. "We'll be on our way."

"Hold on a second. I wasn't born yesterday. What are you up to?" Joe stood before me with his hands on his hips. I wondered if I feinted to the left, he would try to block me.

So I did it, and he did. His reflexes were as sharp as I would expect a fit detective's to be. Mine reflected a great love of sugar, baked goods and appetizers.

I shrugged. "I've seen all there is to see. And you're right. You don't need my help, it doesn't matter exactly how long I was out here because we already know was between five and ten minutes. What difference does it make whether it was six or eight?"

In the moonlight, I could just make out the arching of one eyebrow. "Exactly what I was thinking, but what made you change your mind so quickly?"

I shrugged. "I don't know. Maybe knowing you're here, taking care of things." I gave him my biggest smile. "By the way, Detective, what brings you here? Did somebody request your presence? Or do you make it a habit of cruising past old crime scenes, reliving the excitement?"

I thought he might have been trying to hide a smile. It was pretty dark out there, so I could've been wrong.

"That's my business."

"Fair enough. Then I'll let you get back to it, and we'll get back to ours. As always, it's been a pleasure to see you."

"No offense," he called out to the back of my head as I tried to get away, "but I hope I don't have the pleasure again for a long time."

"Oh, no offense taken. As the same goes double for me." I pulled Raina along beside me, my cheeks burning with embarrassment and barely controlled frustration.

"Be careful of those book club meetings!"

I didn't bother favoring him with a response. It wasn't worth it.

My best friend managed to wait a few minutes before exhaling loudly. "Gosh, it got so hot out there I thought I might have to jump in the pool to cool off." Raina elbowed me in the ribs.

"Oh, hush."

"I'm serious! There was a second there where thought he was gonna reach out and grab you. And not to put hand-cuffs on you, though even that could be fun if done in the right spirit."

"Are you trying to make me furious? Because it's working."

"Lighten up! He's so cute, and you get him all hot and bothered. You know there's a thin line between love and hate."

"Yeah, I'm nowhere near the line. I'm well over into the hate side, thanks very much. I can't imagine anything pushing me over."

She shook her head. "You have no imagination."

"I have plenty of imagination, thank you very much. And you know I do, or you wouldn't keep accusing me of it being overactive." I looked over my shoulder, like I was expecting him to have followed us. That wasn't the case. Even so, when I spoke again, I kept my voice low. "I wonder if my father could find some of the other contracts on file for James's properties in Cape Hope. If he had other part-ners, did they have that same sort of clause, or was it just Robbie and him?"

"Oh, because it sort of looks bad for him if this was a one-time thing, doesn't it?"

"Exactly. I really hope that isn't the case."

"Don't you think the police would've looked into it already?"

I nodded, chewing my lip. Sure, I thought they would've looked into it.

But what I was beginning to understand, slowly but

surely, was that I not only needed to prove Robbie's innocence to potentially save his life.

I need to prove his innocence for myself, too.

I needed to know if I was ever going to be able to sleep
well at night again whether Robert Klein had it in him to
come up with a scheme like this.

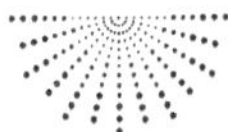

"Emma! It's so nice to see you."

Holly Vaccaro could not be more different from my mother if she tried. Mom was petite, golden-haired, blue-eyed. A peaches and cream complexion. She always spoke gently, her voice lilting like music. Yet at her core was solid steel, evidenced by how hard she'd worked to build a thriving business.

The woman in front of me, a woman who had not yet celebrated her fortieth birthday, was tall and willowy. Olive skinned, with riotous black curls and big, dark eyes. She'd grown up on Staten Island and spoke with a stereotypical twang in her voice. *You* became *yah*, for instance. *It's so nice to see yah.*

Still, she seemed genuine, stepping back from the open door and waving an arm to invite me inside. "Come on in! Your dad's back in the den. He told me you were stopping by. I'm so sorry to hear about what happened with your friend."

"Thanks, I appreciate it." The house they shared was

smaller than the one I grew up in, which Mom still owned. It was closer to the beach, too, and decorated in a bright, breezy theme fitting its location. Lots of blues, tans, a hint of pink and grey. Tasteful, if a little kitschy with all the seashells and lighthouses.

Dad had always loved lighthouses.

She lowered her voice, holding one hand up to the side of her mouth like she was telling me a secret. I couldn't help but take note of the blood red nails that looked like they had been freshly manicured, and the seven or eight bracelets she wore on one wrist. "I bet some of the old gossips around here hounded you for days, didn't they?"

I couldn't help laughing. "Yeah, they did. And still are," I groaned. "It's been a week, for sure."

We came to a stop in the kitchen, where Holly offered something to drink or a snack. "Maybe you could come by for dinner sometime? I always make a pot of gravy on Sundays. I love having it left over in the freezer, but it would be nice to have some more people to eat it with us on Sunday night."

It occurred to me then that Holly might be a little lonely. It probably wasn't easy, coming into Dad's life when most of the town knew everybody else's business. Everybody was aware of and shocked by my parents' divorce when it happened. Not only because there had never been a hint of trouble between them, but because they'd been married for twenty-five years before divorce was even hinted at. It wasn't common for a marriage to last that long, only to end so suddenly.

I suspected Holly received more than her share of side-eye and catty whispers as she went about her grocery shopping. From what I understood, she was a successful interior designer, an entrepreneur in her own right. And she could probably hold her own when it came to standing up for herself.

That was the thing. Nobody in town would come right out and tell her they thought she was a homewrecker. Even if she wasn't, even if she hadn't entered Dad's life until well after the divorce was finalized. They would be civil to her face, but nothing more than that. She couldn't curse them out and tell them what she really thought of them when they weren't outright hostile.

Instead, she had to take it with a smile for Dad's sake. And I believed she would, all for him. She deserved a little friendship. "I would love to. I really would. I'll have to see if I can make it… maybe next weekend?"

And she looked so happy, too. But what she said next really struck me. "I know that would make your father so happy," she whispered.

I was struck with the impulse to hug her, and I did. She squeezed me back, and that felt good. I only wished Darcy would come around. It was easier to let go of grudges.

Dad must've heard our voices and decided he didn't feel like waiting for me. "I got a call from a certain detective in Paradise City earlier today," he announced in a growl. "Can you guess what it was about?"

I winced, rubbing the bridge of my nose. "You might've mentioned that when I called you."

"No, I didn't want to give you an excuse not to show up. You need to be set straight, young lady, and I didn't want you to get out of it."

"She only thinks she's doing what's right," Holly argued

on my behalf, though in a gentle voice. "Just like you would if you were in her place."

"No offense, sweetheart, but this is between Emma and me. I told her in no uncertain terms that I didn't want her getting involved in this, and what does she do?" He turned to me, his face stormy. "She gets herself caught lurking around outside the resort in the dead of night!"

"I was only there to see if I could—"

He held up a hand. "Spare me the explanation. Besides, Sullivan told me all about that himself. Emma, leave it alone. Nobody needs you to be involved in this. The investigation is proceeding the way investigations proceed. End of story."

"Just tell me one thing, please. The reason I called you today in the first place, the reason I came over. Did you ever look at any of the contracts between James Flynn and his other partners here in Cape Hope? He must've had partners, didn't he? Like when he wanted to open the big shopping center that ended up not going anywhere. Remember that?"

Dad looked pained when he nodded. Like he didn't want to admit anything but couldn't help himself. "Yeah, I remember. Of course."

"He was partnered up with a few other people in town, wasn't he? He certainly wasn't funding it by himself. And he must've had some sort of contract with them, an agreement on file somewhere. Did you see any of those? Was there anything included in any of those papers that had to do with what would happen to the partnership in the event that something befell one of the partners? Like an accident or death or illness or something?"

"Most contracts include something like that, sweetie.

That's nothing new. If something happens to one of the partners, the others don't want to be left in the lurch."

"Yeah, but something about this doesn't sit right with me. Is it common for the entire ownership of a project or business or building or anything like that to go straight into the hands of the other partner? Wouldn't it go to the family? Into a trust? Something like that? Why would the other partner retain sole ownership?"

"That does seem like a pretty specific clause," Holly agreed, looking up at Dad. "It's one thing to make allowances in case of an unforeseen event, but..."

He leaned against the sink, looking troubled and more than a little put out by the two of us asking questions at once. "All right, all right. I'll tell you one thing. Yes, all of James Flynn's contracts had that clause attached."

My heart soared. "Really? Then at least the police can't say Robbie planned it all on his own."

"Not so fast," he was quick to counter. "Certainly, it proves it was not Chef Klein's notion, transferring full ownership of the resort to him in the event of James's death. But that doesn't mean he didn't plan this with that in mind. Do you see what I mean?"

Just like that, my heart sank again. "Right."

"What about his other partners?" Holly asked.

"Hon, please." His eyes widened when he stared at her, like he was trying to warn her not to get me started.

But it was too late. I was good and started now. "Yeah! What about those other partners? Did anything ever happen to them? You never did tell me what you found when you were investigating him. Why were you investigating him in the first place? What was it all about?"

"Believe me when I tell you, I have already given the information to the Paradise City Police Department. They are well aware of James Flynn's business history. And if there's anybody who needs to be spoken to, they will have spoken to them by now."

"I haven't spoken to them! And if any of them has any information that could help Robbie, it obviously hasn't been enough to get him out of jail!"

I expected him to yell at me. Or to at least tell me again to mind my own business. Instead, he crossed the kitchen, lowering his hands to my shoulders and looking me straight in the eye. "I know. That's my point. Nobody has information that's enough to clear your friend of these charges."

"They're just not asking the right questions, that's all." I stared up at him, unblinking. "I will not believe he is guilty. I can't. I know he didn't do this."

His head lowered, swinging back and forth. "I wish there was something I could say to get through to you. I just want you to prepare yourself for the very real possibility that Robbie is not going to be cleared of this."

"Don't you want to help him if he's innocent? Don't you care?"

"Sure, honey. I care. But I care more about you, and I see how worked up you are over this. It pains me, truly it does. You're my daughter. You're always going to come first."

I leaned against him, heartsick and sad. Poor Robbie was in jail and I knew he didn't do it. I was as certain as could be. "Do you think I could visit him?"

"I don't know, honey."

"Please, could you see?" There I was. The girl who got annoyed when anybody suggested she should listen to her father. Begging my father for help. "Maybe pull a few strings? You gave them all that information you'd put together down here, regarding James's business records. They owe you one, don't they?"

He chuckled. "It doesn't work like that. Not really."

"Oh, come on," Holly insisted.

I had the feeling this was partially a ploy to get on my good side, but I was willing to accept all the help I could get. Besides, I'd never felt as strongly about her as Darcy had. The woman had a good heart, and she loved my dad. That was enough for me.

"How am I supposed to refuse you both?" he asked. I had the feeling he wasn't as irritated as he pretended to be. Maybe he liked seeing the two of us on the same team. "All right. I'll make a phone call. But don't expect miracles."

"I won't," I promised, even as my hopes soared.

CHAPTER TWENTY-THREE

After popping a container of Holly's sauce—gravy, as she called it—in the microwave, I set water on to boil for pasta. Part of me felt a little guilty for eating Holly's cooking, knowing how much Mom still missed Dad even if she didn't like to admit it.

And I could never tell Darcy. Never, ever. Not until she got over the sense that Dad was somehow being unfaithful to Mom by moving on with his life.

But Holly meant well, really she did. Dad loved her, even if she was his polar opposite. She brought him happiness. The least I could do was test her sauce and come to dinner.

It was Thirsty Thursday to those members of the human race with social lives, and I heard a handful of people laughing as they crossed the street beneath my window. Deke's question of whether I had friends my own age tugged at the back of my mind, and I wished Raina wasn't living in Manhattan and always jetting off to fabulous locations so she could write about her travels and accommodations.

Maybe I did need some more friends. Nobody could replace Raina, naturally, but I couldn't spend my life alone when she was busy with a life of her own. Texting wasn't the same as having somebody to get a drink or see a movie with.

Now that nearly three weeks had passed since the breakup, it was time to start getting myself back together. I would reach out to old friends and let them know I was alive and well, that they didn't have to avoid me like I carried a contagious disease.

Just having this on the horizon was enough to pick up my mood.

So, too, was the ringing of my phone as I poured rigatoni into salted, boiling water—not so much the ringing, but the knowledge of who was calling.

Not that Deke made me happy in any way, shape, or form. I was just glad to hear from him because we were supposed to get together to look over his pictures again. "Tell me you came back early," I begged, stirring the pasta.

"Hello to you, too. Miami is beautiful. Thanks for asking."

I growled. "You're still there."

"If I didn't know better, I'd think you missed me. But I most definitely know better." He chuckled. "Sorry to disappoint you. But I did wanna check in since it's been a couple of days. Knowing you, you've managed to get yourself into trouble at least once."

"I did not!"

"All right. If not trouble, at least a sticky situation."

I hesitated, eyes squeezing shut. "Nope. I haven't."

"Liar, liar, pants on fire."

"It wasn't such a big deal. And actually, I wanted to tell you about it." I gave him the rundown of what I'd learned about the resort opening. "So it looks like things are gonna move ahead. A little later than originally planned, since it was supposed to be open to guests this week, but still."

"Maybe Haute Cuisine will give the go-ahead to keep moving, then," he suggested.

"I left a message for Marsha earlier today and am just waiting for her to get back to me. I'd imagine she wants to verify, make sure I'm not pulling her leg."

"Of course."

"I think my dad's going to arrange a visit with Robbie."

"Oh, Emma."

"What?" I demanded. "Are you going to tell me it's a bad idea, too? Because I'm pretty sure if his girlfriend hadn't pestered him for me, he would never have agreed."

"He's a smart man."

"Robbie's my friend. Or he was. Wouldn't you want to see a friendly face if you were in such an awful position?"

"Sure, especially if that person was only there to be friendly. But you and I both know you're not just being friendly."

"I want to see if he's okay. And yes, fine, sure. I wanna ask if he's thought of anything since Friday that might cast a new light on things. I mean, he was probably in shock. Who can think clearly after something so terrible happens? Now that he's had a few days to process the event, he might have come up with a bunch of information nobody wants to listen to."

"You have a way of infuriating people, you know that?

And not because you're unlikable. Just the opposite. I wish I didn't like you, so I wouldn't care."

I blinked, going still with a wooden spoon in my hand. "Huh?"

"What?"

"You said you like me?" It was barely a squeak.

"Well, I don't hate you. Did you think I hated you?"

"You were pretty rude at first."

"That's not the first time I've been called rude," he admitted, sounding rueful. "I don't mean to be. When I'm in the zone, camera in hand, I tend to forget everything around me. It isn't intentional. And it's not personal."

"Good to know." I couldn't get my pulse under control. It was all fluttery and uneven. He liked me? No, not like that. Right?

"Like I was saying," he went on after clearing his throat, "I don't want to see you walking into something that might cause you grief. Even if Robert's innocent, what if you never find something to prove his innocence? What if the murderer thought of everything?"

"There's no such thing as a perfect murder," I reminded him. "There's always a slip-up somewhere. The killer always makes a mistake."

"And you know that because…?"

"Because everybody knows that, of course."

"So why are there so many unsolved homicides on the books? A detective's daughter should know that. A criminal justice student should know it, too."

I was about to boil over like the pasta water, which I took off the heat before draining in the sink. "Okay, okay. I should've known I would get an attitude. But don't think you can dissuade me from stalking you until I get another look at your photos. There's gotta be something. You took so many."

"Which you made a snide remark about at the time."

"I'll take it all back if you have something on that memory card that proves someone else drugged James."

He sighed softly. "You're impossible. I'll be back on Saturday. I can drive in to see you, if you want."

His choice of words stirred something in my core that I didn't want to be stirred up. But there was no helping it. "Yeah. Okay. Give me a call then and we'll set a time."

"Great. In the meantime, be good."

I stuck my tongue out, even though he couldn't see, before tossing my pasta with some of Holly's sauce. "Holy cow, this is terrific," I said to no one, my mouth full.

I definitely could not tell my sister about this. It would kill her to know Holly was good in the kitchen.

The phone rang again, and this time it was my dad.

"Whoa, Dad," I said, taking another bite even though it was rude to do so while on the phone. "I'm amazed by this sauce! And I'm definitely coming for dinner soon if it means getting more."

"Aw, sweetie. That'll make Holly so happy. She really wants to be friends with you girls."

I grimaced. "Well, she might have to wait a little while for Darcy to come around. I'll try to warm her up as best I can."

"Your sister's a stubborn kid," he murmured. "She needs time, I guess. Even if it's been two years since I got together with Holly."

"I'll do my best," I promised. "Especially if you tell me you got permission for me to speak with Robbie."

"He's not supposed to be seeing anybody but his lawyer and his wife right now," Dad reminded me, and the sauce went sour in my mouth. "But I got you ten minutes with him tomorrow afternoon."

"Dad! You're the best!"

"That's ten minutes, young lady. No more. Ten. You can't pass him anything, you can't bring him any gifts. You'll have to go through a metal detector."

"Sure, of course." My head was already spinning. Ten minutes. I'd have to come up with the right questions in advance so as to not waste time.

"And don't be upset or disappointed if he doesn't want to speak with you."

That knocked me for a loop. "Why wouldn't he want to?"

"Think about all the strain he's been under, honey. He's frightened, I'm sure. Confused. Wondering how this happened to him. Embarrassed, more than likely. I've seen it happen more times than I can count, and I've watched family members and close friends weeping because they don't understand why their loved one won't see them. Sometimes, it's a way to protect the ones they care about."

"I get it."

"Sure, you get it now. But you might feel differently in the moment. I'm just trying to warn you not to get your hopes up too high."

"It seems like everybody shares that opinion lately," I confessed.

"Maybe if enough people warn you, you'll listen." He snickered. "Then again, I know who I'm talking to."

"Ha, ha."

"Two o'clock tomorrow."

"I'll be there. Thanks, Dad."

"Don't thank *me*. Not entirely."

"What do you mean?"

"Your buddy, Detective Sullivan, gave the green light. You should thank him. I'm sure his superiors are breathing down his neck."

"He's not—" No, that wouldn't sound right.

My father would jump on my insisting I clarify that we were not, in fact, buddies. He might not have been the well-meaning busybody Mom was, but he knew how to embarrass his daughter when he put his mind to it. A dad superpower.

I settled for grunting. "Hmph. Okay. I'll thank him when I see him." Since something told me he'd make a point of rubbing in my face that he was the big hero, anyway.

It didn't matter. I had to focus on getting the most out of my time with Robbie as possible. There were so many things I wanted to know.

CHAPTER TWENTY-FOUR

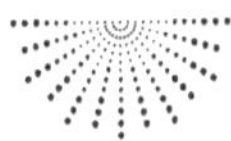

"Why won't you tell me where you're going this afternoon?" Mom insisted on shadowing me around the café. That's what I got for offering to help her out, to make up for cutting out early on Sunday.

Though as far as I was concerned, I'd more than made up for that by fielding questions for an hour at her house during Book Club.

When it doubt, deflect with tales of baked goods. "Did I tell you I made excellent lemon bars over the weekend? I think they'd be a great addition to the spring menu." I was already mentally calculating the number of lemons we'd need while carrying a pan of dirty mugs and plates to the kitchen.

Even the promise of tart-tangy-sweet bars kissed with powdered sugar did nothing to dissuade her, as she followed me straight to the sink. "Emma!"

"Mom!" I mimicked with a grin. "It's not that important. I just need to leave around one-fifteen. That's all. I have an appointment."

"Oh, no." She fell back, one hand over her chest. "You're sick. That's what you don't want to tell me. There something wrong with you, and you're trying to spare me."

"Mom. I'm fine. There is absolutely nothing wrong with me, I'm in perfect health" Then, something even worse than being hounded over meeting with Robbie occurred to me. "Please, do not say a word about my being sick to anybody in the café. Promise?"

By the time I got home, there would be a candlelit prayer vigil taking place on the sidewalk outside the pizza shop. Maybe Mr. Angelo would see a nice boost in business from it, but he'd be the only one benefitting.

"So long as you promise you're being honest with me about being healthy," she sniffed.

The woman was mad as a hatter, but I loved her. I gave her a quick hug and a kiss on the cheek. "I promise. You have the wrong idea entirely."

She followed me back out into the dining area, cornering me behind the counter. "So? Why won't you share? What could possibly be so important that you couldn't share it with your mother?"

My nerves were thin enough after a long night spent going over everything I wanted to ask my old friend, then fretting that he wouldn't want to speak to me at all. This was not the time for my mother to be dancing the cha-cha on the last nerve I had left.

"Mom, no offense, but you have a tendency to blow things out of proportion," I whispered as gently as I could.

She gasped like I had just insulted her double chocolate chip cookies. And I would never, ever, do such a terrible thing because they were iconic.

"Me? Blow things out of proportion?"

"I find it ironic that you're practically swooning over this. Don't you see the irony? Look at it from my perspective." I chuckled to myself, turning my attention to rearranging the baked goods in the case so they look a little more attractive. The early morning rush had already come and gone, and now all that was left was cleaning up after the madness and settling in for the usual, steadily busy day ahead.

"I don't think this is funny. You always want to laugh at me, or make me out to be silly or frivolous, but I truly worry about you."

"Mom, there's nothing to worry about!"

"That's easy for you to say. After you were at an event last week where a murder took place."

I looked across the café to one of the pastel tables currently occupied by a young mother and her two children. The kids hadn't heard, but their mother had. And she did not look thrilled.

"Mom," I whispered, nodding toward the trio.

Mom grimaced embarrassment, shrugging, mouthing her apologies.

Then she turned back to me, whispering now. "I don't see how you can expect me to pretend everything's all right when something terrible could've happened to you that night. You were in a room with a murderer."

"I know. But nothing did happen to me, and nothing is going to."

"It's going to bother me terribly if you don't at least hint at what you're doing today. Wouldn't you feel terrible if something happened while you weren't here? What if I had an accident? What if the last thing you never did was upset me?"

"Oh, please. Can we not get into this right now? I'm not sure I can stand the guilt." One of the timers went off in the kitchen, and I had never been so glad to have an excuse to go back there.

She followed me anyway, even if there were guests currently seated out in the dining room. "Since when do we keep secrets from each other?"

I paused in the act of removing two pans of blueberry muffins from the oven just long enough to roll my eyes. "That's the problem, Mom. I tell you things, and you end up telling half the town. You should know better by now."

"I do not!"

"No? For instance, you told Frankie Pierce that Deke was my gentleman friend. That's not true. In fact, we're not even friends in the platonic sense. We're colleagues, nothing more. Now, everybody thinks I moved on from Landon too quickly, and I'm dating somebody else. Do you know how uncomfortable that makes me? I would think that after watching me being grilled on Tuesday, you'd have a sense of what you put me through. I know you don't mean to do it, but it happens."

Her eyelids fluttered. "Does this mean you won't tell me anything anymore? Is that it?"

I gave her another hug. "Of course not. But you have to forgive me if certain things need to be kept private. I need to have some semblance of my own private life. It's not easy, growing up in a town where everybody knows you."

The bell jingled over the front door, and Mom made a hasty exit to greet a new customer. I was glad for a momentary reprieve, the chance to take a breath and remind myself that healthy boundaries were a good thing. I needed more of them in my life.

Starting with keeping certain parts of my life to myself. Clearly, reminding my mother not to spread my business around did nothing. No matter what I told her, she insisted on doing her own thing.

It didn't help that the first person who came to mind was Joe Sullivan. Hadn't he accused me of something like that on Tuesday? With that little crack he made about my being inebriated, and that maybe I would listen better under the influence since I didn't when I was sober.

Now, I sounded just like him. It was almost enough to make me stress-eat a blueberry muffin. Good thing they were piping hot and would probably burn my mouth.

"Emma! There's something out here for you."

I poked my head out the swinging door to find Trixie Graham chatting with my mother. She was somewhere between the ages of thirty-five and sixty. I never could quite pin her down. She and my mother were thick as thieves, and along with my Auntie Nell were troublemakers, to put it mildly.

She waved a small, white envelope in the air, removing a big pair of sunglasses which she thought made her look like Jackie Onassis. They did not. "Yours is the pink Bug outside, isn't it?"

I nodded, holding my hand out. "What, was that under the wiper?"

With her free hand, she tapped her forefinger to her nose. "I thought that was your car. I was afraid perhaps someone had dinged it on the way past and left their information, but I didn't see any damage." Yes, and knowing Trixie, she would've gone over it with a magnifying glass. She had a nose for news, a reputation she enjoyed as one of the senior reporters for the *Times*.

At least the envelope was sealed, telling me she hadn't tampered with it. Not that I believed her to have anything but the best intentions, but she was the biggest snoop in town. Always trying to get the scoop. No doubt she had already grilled my mother outside my presence.

I turned my back, opening the envelope and unfolding the slip of paper inside. What did I expect to find? I hadn't considered it.

Which was why I was completely unprepared for what was inside, written in block letters.

WATCH YOUR BACK

I took a glance over my shoulder, where my mom and Trixie were, of course, pretending not to be deathly curious over what I'd just opened. At least they weren't reading along with me. "I have to make a phone call."

Who was I going to call? I could call Dad, but he would just tell me this was one more reason to stay out of the investigation. Was it even related to the investigation, though? I didn't know. Why else would I have to watch my back?

And why would anybody in Cape Hope care?

I had to tell somebody about this, though. I'd burst if I had to keep it to myself. Raina was on a flight to Barbados and wouldn't be back until Monday.

"Don't make me regret this, Deke," I whispered as I

waited for him to answer, huddled in the back corner of the kitchen. I had to position myself as far as I could from the swinging door and hope neither mom nor Trixie was listening from the alley. It was just the sort of thing they would do.

"Hello? Deke's phone."

Why did the sound of a woman's voice startle me so badly? Because I'd expected it to be Deke, of course. That was all. Nothing more than that. "Um. Hi. Sorry. I was calling for Deke. Obviously. Sorry." Great, and now whoever she was would think I was deeply disturbed and unable to express myself.

"He's in the shower at the moment. Can I tell him who's calling and have him call you back?"

Gosh darn it, why did my stomach clench and my chest tighten and my eyes water? What, did I expect him to be pining over me? Living a chaste life in hopes of winning my heart one day? Of course not! I didn't even like him like that.

"Uh, sure. It's Emma Harmon. It's—I mean, I can tell him why I called when he calls back. But it's not an emergency or anything."

"Okay. I'll tell him you called, Emma. Have a good one!" Whoever she was, she had perkiness down pat. I had a hard time seeing Deke with a perky girl, since he was about the furthest from perky of anybody I'd ever met.

But opposites did attract. Look at Dad and Holly, who were on opposite ends of the spectrum in every way and deeply in love.

I didn't know if I was more stricken over the note or Miss Perky as I hugged myself in the corner of the kitchen, eyeing the blueberry muffins and rationalizing the eating of just one. One wouldn't make a difference.

Someday, I'd have to learn healthy ways to deal with stress which didn't involve baked goods. I wouldn't always have a high metabolism.

No, a muffin wouldn't help. I looked at the note again, wondering who could've left it. And exactly what I was supposed to be watching out for.

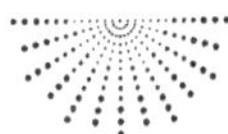

CHAPTER TWENTY-FIVE

"There she is. My favorite wannabe sleuth." Joe Sullivan was grinning in a humorless way when I stepped into the jailhouse. He was sprawled casually on a wooden bench, waiting for me, and stood when I approached.

I barely kept from rolling my eyes at his rudeness. "I sure was hoping you'd be here today," I managed with a sickly-sweet smile. "I wanted to thank you in person for making this possible."

"Who said I made anything possible?"

"My dad, of course. He said I had you to thank."

"He's too generous." Joe tossed a coffee stirrer into the trash, and I couldn't help but look as we passed the basket. Sure enough, he'd chewed it to bits. Was he still worried about the case?

"Well, I do thank you. This means a lot." I followed him past rows of cubicles, nodding to a few people we passed. They didn't know me, and I didn't know them, but when somebody stared at me, I couldn't help but react.

Or maybe they were staring at him. Heck, I'd stare at him, too.

We walked down a flight of stairs. "I take it your father gave you the rundown. Ten minutes. No more."

"Got it." I bit back a retort, something sarcastic, knowing it would only mean pressing my luck. This wasn't the time to be sassy.

He looked me up and down, and for a second, I thought he was sizing up my sundress and sandals. No, he just wanted to be sure I wasn't bringing anything to Robbie. "No weapons?"

"No weapons. Do you want to search my bag?" I held it out to him. "You can."

He considered it, then shook his head. "No, I trust you."

"You do? Wow. I feel like I should record that for posterity."

He was chuckling as we reached a green, metal door with a window in the center. Two panes of what I guessed was unbreakable glass with metal wiring in between. "I've got to admit, you're more amusing than the people in my office."

For a second, I considered telling him about the note under my windshield. It burned a hole in my purse, on the forefront of my mind. But there was nothing he could do about it. Besides, I still didn't know exactly what it meant or what I was supposed to be watching out for.

"You all right?" My expression must've shifted when I thought about the note, reflecting how conflicted it left me. "Not getting cold feet, are you?"

"My feet are warm, thanks."

"Because you don't have to do this if you're nervous."

"I'm not nervous!"

"You look nervous."

"If I do, it's because you're pestering me."

"If you say so," he shrugged before opening the door, nodding to a pair of guards. I nodded, too, before I could ask myself why in the world I was nodding. I felt like I should do something. Maybe I should've been sedated before this, since I clearly couldn't handle myself.

He led me down a narrow corridor lined in doors painted the same drab shade of olive green. "You'll be in the room at the end," he explained, pointing. "Glass separating you, of course."

I decided not to remind him at that moment that I did, in fact, understand how this worked. He was nice for once and he was technically doing me a favor. Even I knew better than to look a gift horse in the mouth.

"Okay," I murmured, my palms slick with nervous sweat.

Just because I knew how it worked didn't mean I wasn't nervous as anything. No matter how many times I told Joe I wasn't.

He opened the last door, revealing little more than a cubby with a shallow shelf running underneath the glass wall separating it from the cubby on the other side. I took a seat on a metal chair and waited with my hands folded in my lap while Joe waited outside the door. I guessed he was a necessary evil I couldn't get rid of.

The opening of the door on the other side of the glass made me forget Joe and even the note in my purse for a moment. The sight of Robert Klein, a rising star in the culinary world, made the breath catch in my throat.

He looked tired. So tired. Like a decade had passed since

I saw him only a week earlier. The tan shirt and pants he wore—government issued, of course—only highlighted the sickly pallor of his skin. The light in his eyes had extinguished.

Yet he managed a gentle smile when he sat across from me, on the other side of that glass wall. "You didn't have to come," he murmured.

"Sure, I did. I've been thinking of you all this time, hoping there was some way I could help."

"There isn't any," he whispered. "They're convinced it was me."

"I know it wasn't."

"You would be one of the only people who do." He sighed with a slight shake of his head. "I don't even think Aubrey believes me anymore. She's going ahead with the opening. Did you know that?"

"Sure. I saw it for myself. They're getting things moving again."

There I was, thinking he'd be happy the opening was continuing without him. I guessed there was only so much enthusiasm a person could show when they were handcuffed and facing the possibility of prison.

"It's a good thing, of course. Everybody's counting on their jobs."

"But you deserve to be there, working alongside them."

He shrugged, looking so hopeless. "I thought I would be. I don't know what went wrong."

I remembered the ticking clock and the questions I needed to ask. We were already wasting valuable time. "Robbie, were you having issues with James Flynn before that night? You said something to me before the doors opened about not letting James fool me. He wanted to project a certain image, but you seemed to know better. What did that mean?"

He snorted. "He grew up on the streets but wanted everybody to think he had this rare pedigree. Sure, he got involved in real estate at an early age and probably swindled a ton of people to get where he ended up. I heard a story about a guy he worked for in New York having half his clients stolen by James, after James got fired from the firm for shady practices."

"You heard that, but you still wanted to work with him?"

"I didn't know about it—any of it—until after the ink had dried on the paperwork. Oh, Emma. I was such a fool. He saw me coming a mile away. I might as well have a bullseye painted on my back. He knew I wanted that restaurant more than anything in the world, and he drew me in with promises of success. He knew how to run a hotel, he told me, and I believed him. I'm sure he had skill. But he was better at lying."

"When did you find out about all of this?"

"Roughly a month before we were due to open. I didn't say anything to him. I did my homework, though. Asking questions, studying the books more closely. In short, he was a magician. Making numbers magically do what he wanted them to do. None of it made sense. I finally asked him about it a week prior to the opening, when I had what I considered enough proof."

"And?"

"And he asked what I intended to do about it. We had already sunk a ton of money into the project—my life savings, for one, not to mention loans I took out to finance the rest. He pointed out how much I stood to lose and reminded me that his business was his, while mine was mine. I needed to focus on the restaurant and let him do what he did best. Only I couldn't. Could you?"

I realized he was truly asking me this question, looking for a response. I shook my head. "No way."

"I asked a few more questions during that impromptu meeting," he confessed. "And found out what I'd suspected was true. He was a complete illusion, top to bottom. In debt up to his eyeballs. I decided I didn't want to have anything more to do with him if I could help it. So I got a lawyer and had her draw up paperwork disengaging me from James Flynn. I wanted no part of him anymore. She assured me I could claim ours was a bad faith agreement. I gave him the papers that night, before the opening."

I almost fell off my chair. "He carried them in his pocket, didn't he?"

"I think so. Yes. In his jacket, now that I picture it in my head."

"How did he take it? When you gave them to him?"

"It wasn't as if I was handing him a certified check, you know. He was furious. Enraged. But we had to put on a happy face. Maybe I should've waited until after the event, but I couldn't help myself. I needed him to know that I was onto him."

And those papers were missing. At least, they weren't in his jacket when I stumbled across his body. "Did anybody else know you were doing this?"

"I told Aubrey. She deserved to know. I didn't tell her why, though. I tried to keep her out of it. I knew she would only be upset if she found out what a fool I was to let James sucker me in. I was the legitimate face of his business, you know? And I wouldn't have been surprised if he'd planned to leave me holding the bag once everything went south."

"How did she take it when you told her?"

He shrugged. "She didn't really understand. I told her the restaurant would still continue to operate, but we wouldn't be sharing any of the profits from the resort itself. Just the restaurant. What was ours was ours, what was his was his. I was doing this to protect us. I mean, considering how indebted he was to just about everybody up and down the coastline, I figured this was the best way to keep from losing everything. She was grateful that I was handling it. She even made me out to be a hero, like I was clever enough to disengage when I didn't quite trust him." His head sank between his shoulders. "A hero. An idiot, more like. A sucker."

"You weren't a sucker. You were looking for a way to get what you wanted. Your dream. There's nothing wrong with that. He was wrong for taking advantage of you. I know he did it before, to other people. I only wish he'd gotten what he deserved before he did it to you."

I realized what I'd just said and how it could be misconstrued. "I mean, not that I wish he was killed before. But arrested. Prosecuted."

"I know what you meant," he assured me with a ghost of a smile.

How much time did we have left? I should've time us but dropped the ball. "How are you holding up? What's your lawyer think about this?"

"It's not looking good," he admitted. "At least I know this can still move on without me. Aubrey will sell the resort or bring a management company on. One or the other. She can't possibly do everything on her own. And Kyle will manage the restaurant while this is all worked out. I can only hope justice will prevail. I didn't kill him, Emma."

"I know you didn't."

"I wish everybody else did. Not even my own wife believes me. I can see it in her eyes, no matter how upbeat she tries to appear. She's coming in later today. I can't believe I dread seeing her, but I do."

"She loves you. She wants to support you." But I remembered what Dad told me, too. Many people in Robbie's position would rather avoid their loved ones.

Joe rapped on the door, signaling the end of our time together. I didn't want to leave him in this place, looking so sad, feeling hopeless. "I'm doing everything I can for you, Robbie."

"What can you do?" he asked with a flat chuckle. "Unless you're smarter than every investigator on the case. Which I guess is possible."

"I won't stop trying. I promise." I turned, prepared to leave with a heavy heart, when one more question popped up. "Was James on any medication you're aware of?"

He frowned. "I don't think so."

Darn it. I was hoping for a clue as to how he might've been drugged.

"Stay strong," I whispered, pressing my fingers to my lips and blowing him a kiss before leaving with tears in my eyes.

If Joe noticed, he was nice enough not to say anything.

Though I knew I wasn't imagining his hand resting against my back as we walked down the door-lined corridor, away from poor Robbie.

"Emma? Emma!"

I paused in the act of unlocking my door, looking around to see who'd called my name. I wanted to get far away from that jailhouse. What did I think I was going to accomplish besides breaking my own heart?

The sight of red hair attached to a stylish young woman only made my heart sink lower than ever. Poor Aubrey, trying to hold everything together while her husband sat in jail, awaiting trial. I waved with a smile. Only to find her unwilling to return my smile.

"I'm sorry," she murmured on reaching me, "but what is there between you and my husband?"

"What?" I laughed. It wasn't funny, not in the least, but that was how my surprise came out. In the form of an ill-timed laugh.

"You think this is funny?" she demanded, arms folded, looking me up and down like I was some sort of challenge. Terrific. I'd managed to make her angrier.

"Aubrey, please. No. There's nothing between Robert and me. I came as a friend to see him. Nothing more."

"Just like you so happened to run into my brother in the park the other day."

"I didn't know he was your brother at the time. I did just so happen to see him, and I remembered him from the kitchen. That's all."

She was not about to be calmed. "You say you aren't writing an article about this, but you can't stay away. Which tells me you're either lying about that, or you're lying about your feelings for my husband."

"I hadn't seen him in ten years. Please, you have the wrong idea. I only want to see justice served. Don't you want as many people on your side as possible? And we are on the same side, I promise."

She was just upset, overwrought as anybody would be under the circumstances.

She hesitated, looking me over again, before deflating like a balloon. "I'm sorry. Really. I'm just so tired and heartsick."

"I can't imagine. But you're handling things so well. I'm sure Robert is proud of you." Calling him Robbie would get me nowhere fast, I had a feeling.

She grimaced. "Now I can see why he was so stressed out leading up to the opening. I thought he was acting strange. Especially while getting almost no sleep. His back started acting up, probably from stress. No wonder he took so many pills."

I could practically hear a record scratching in my head. "Excuse me?"

"Pain medication, you know. The stress had him hurting

all over. At least the meds helped his mood at first. Now I understand why he needed them so badly. I wish I had some myself, to be honest." She rubbed her temples. "My head is splitting from morning til night."

My head bobbed up and down. Sure, yeah, totally normal. Confessing to a stranger that her husband was popping pain meds in the days leading up to the opening. Was this her way of easing me into the idea that Robbie was out of his mind when he killed James?

Was Robbie right when he said she might believe he was the killer?

Or was she only exhausted and traumatized, as any loving wife would be? After all, she was coming to visit him. She was devoted to him.

"I can assure you," I said after I found my voice, "that I'm only trying to help. I wanted him to know he has friends on his side who believe in him. I hope I managed to make him feel just a smidge better. I don't expect miracles. But I'm thinking about him, and about you."

"Thank you, Emma." She surprised me by giving me an impulsive hug—hard, fierce, practically crushing my ribs. "I should get in there. He's probably waiting for me."

"Of course." I went back to opening the car door and slid inside, starting up upon settling in. But I didn't pull away immediately. I lingered, watching Aubrey walk into the building.

Something about her didn't sit right with me.

The ringing of my phone gave me a start, but it reminded me that I didn't have all day to sit and stare at a building, either. Life rolled on, the way I needed to be doing. I answered through the hands-free system installed in the car stereo as I pulled out of the parking lot. "Hello?"

"Emma? Did you call earlier? Sorry I was unavailable."

Deke. My stomach lurched. "Oh, yeah. I almost forgot." But now it all came back with a sickening thud. The surprise of hearing a girl answer his phone. The surprise that I cared in the least.

"Everything okay?"

"Uh, it wasn't at the time, but I might've been blowing things out of proportion. You know me. Typical Emma." I let out a hollow laugh.

"What's wrong with you?" he asked. "You sound funny."

"I'm driving."

"That's not what I mean. You sound like you're upset. What's going on?"

"I visited Robbie," I blurted out rather than asking who the girl on the phone was.

"You did? How is he?"

"Terrible, of course. You know what those papers were in James's jacket? Some sort of legal stuff Robbie gave him that very night, something that would break their partnership. He found out James was a crook and wanted to disengage so he wasn't left holding the bag if the ship sank."

"No kidding! And somebody took them?"

"Looks like it. So who would stand to lose the most if that went through? Robbie only served to gain from it. Everybody in the entire restaurant served to gain, because it would give them stability in the long run."

"Maybe someone didn't understand that."

"Hmm. You're right, I guess. No matter which way I look, it's just as murky in all directions."

"You need a break from all of this."

I laughed. "Says the guy who's in Florida, enjoying fun in the sun."

"I'm not in Miami anymore."

"You're home?" I wished I didn't sound so hopeful, but after all, I wanted another look at those pictures.

"Not quite. Visiting family. My sister says you sound nice over the phone."

His sister? His sister! Dang it, why did that make me so happy? "She sounds nice, too. So you have a family. You didn't magically spring up out of nowhere one day?" Even my voice sounded lighter. I could hear it myself.

"Who said I did?"

"Nobody, but you've never mentioned them." I paused. "Or how much wealth you come from."

It was his turn to pause. "So you've been digging."

"You weren't the only one who was curious," I reminded him. "And you do owe me one. Remember? I told you outside my apartment."

"Just because you decide I owe you one doesn't mean I owe you one. What difference does it make who my family is?"

"No difference at all. I find it interesting that you never speak of them."

"Not everybody is so open to pouring out their life story to virtual strangers."

"Pardon? Forgive me, but that was pretty rude." And there I was, thinking we'd come so far.

"It isn't any of your business. It's not anybody's business. Did it ever occur to you that I might want something for myself? Something not attached to my family?"

"Not until you just said it now," I admitted.

"What if everyone you knew assumed you'd follow in your mother's footsteps? Or in your father's?"

"It would aggravate me. And it has, lots of times."

"Imagine having a name people recognized outside your town. Extrapolate that. How would it make you feel?"

"I get it. I don't see why you have to take it out on me, though."

"I wasn't trying to. I don't know what I was trying to do."

There was an uneasy silence between us as I continued my way down the turnpike. "Anything else? Or can I get back to driving?" I asked.

"Do you still want to get together and look at the photos tomorrow?"

"I don't know. I'm starting to think this is completely hopeless."

"I don't believe it is."

"That makes me feel a lot better. I'm starting to wonder if Aubrey isn't shielding her brother somehow. It's too big a coincidence, him being an ex-convict and all. He had a lot to lose if the restaurant went under, but he probably wouldn't have known the intricacies of the problems between Robbie and James. He might've assumed them breaking their part-nership would be the end of the road."

I snickered. "Or maybe I'm just kidding myself."

"Maybe you do need a break from this."

"But that's just it, Deke. That's what nobody under-stands. Robbie doesn't get a break from it. And it pains me, it really does, to think of him being so hopeless."

He sighed. "I wish I could offer something that would

help, aside from urging you to take some time for yourself. I'll call you tomorrow, okay?"

"Yeah. Okay." Because we weren't friends, so it didn't matter that he'd hurt my feelings and there was nothing stopping us from getting together to talk about something work-related.

"And Emma?" he asked just as I was about to end the call and maybe scream and curse a little.

"Yeah?"

"I'm sorry. I shouldn't have snapped. It's a touchy subject, is all. But you didn't deserve that."

Okay, so maybe he made up for it a little with that apology. "I get it. Sorry for stepping where I shouldn't step, too. Talk to you tomorrow."

I wished I could shake the feeling of there being something I was missing as I cruised down the turnpike, heading home, knowing my mother would grill me up and down over where I'd been.

If anything, I would gladly withstand it so long as I could get a hug.

CHAPTER TWENTY-SEVEN

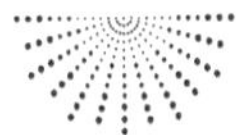

"So let's get this straight." The image on my phone's screen was of Raina in a white bikini, sitting in a lounge chair with the bluest sky I'd ever seen behind her. Sunglasses covered half her face and her skin was shiny thanks to sunscreen and probably perspiration after hours in the tropical sun.

Anybody in the world would've rested and relaxed and thanked their lucky stars to be in paradise. My best friend, on the other hand, wanted to help me solve this mystery.

Which of course was why we were best friends.

"Aubrey has sole control over the business now," she mused, staring past the phone. I imagined it was a pristine, white-sand beach in front of her.

"Right. I guess so." I leaned over my kitchen counter, reaching for the powdered sugar. Stress baking was second only to stress eating in my book, and I wanted a fresh batch of lemon bars to take to Mom and prove they were worthy of selling in the café.

"And she said Robbie was popping pills in the days leading up to the opening."

"Which is just something she said," I pointed out. "We don't know that's a fact."

"Right, but still. Why would she randomly say that? What if she's doubting him and needed to get that off her chest?"

"I wish I knew." I watched powdered sugar sift over the delightfully yellow bars. They were so cheerful, so pretty.

"Hmm." She tapped a finger to her chin. "What if Kyle did it, and she's shielding him?"

"That's exactly what I said to Deke!" I would've whooped with joy if the idea wasn't completely morbid and inappropriate. Having Raina draw the same conclusion I had was a relief, though. I couldn't help it.

"Yeah, because he wouldn't know the specifics of what was going on, unless Robbie told him. Why would he? Kyle didn't need to know. If he didn't tell his own wife, he wouldn't have told his brother-in-law."

"Precisely. Kyle might've heard them talking about legal stuff, business stuff. I mean, he was there in the restaurant probably the entire time Robbie and James were. Or maybe Aubrey told him about it as a heads up. He knew James was carrying the papers and he took them after the stabbing."

"And he probably figured Aubrey would take control of the business! That would set her up, wouldn't it? He did it for her, too!"

We stared at each other, hundreds of miles apart.

"Are we basing this off speculation and theory?" she asked.

"We are. We're probably way off-base."

"Is that going to stop you from pursuing this?"

"Probably not."

"Why do I have to be all the way down here right now? I don't trust you looking into this on your own, without me to keep you from taking too many chances."

"What's the big deal? Maybe I'll take some of these lemon bars over to Kyle's apartment as a gift. You know, the way people do in times of trouble. And maybe, I don't know, I'll ask if he's into stabbing people."

"Em."

"You know I wouldn't." But I couldn't help considering it. It wasn't a bad idea, using food as an excuse to get another few minutes with him. Completely innocent. "Besides, he's probably at the restaurant, working. Not at home. I'd have to take them to the restaurant."

"Would you please not? Or at least wait until I get home?"

"Raina…" I pouted. "I won't get into any trouble."

"The guy could be a murderer. You're acting on the theory that he is a straight-up murderer."

"Okay. Fine. What if I reach out to Aubrey, then? A way of saying I don't hold it against her that she basically called me a wannabe homewrecker today? I bring the lemon bars, we chat about her brother, bing-bang-boom."

"I don't like it."

"And I'm impatient. Don't worry, everything will be okay. I'll call you after, I swear. Go inside. You're starting to get all freckled."

"Am I?" she asked, looking down at her flawless skin.

"No. Perfect as always. Talk soon." I ended the call before

she could give me any further reason why driving up to the resort was a bad idea.

"Mmm," I groaned, taking a bite of one of the bars. "You're almost too good to give away."

I was only a couple of minutes from the resort, driving with a plate of lemon bars beside me and the newly relit Riviera sign beckoning me up ahead, when the ringing of my phone blared out in my little car. It always shocked me when my music stopped and instead of soft rock from the eighties, an electronic ringing noise sounded.

"Hello?"

"Emma. It's Deke. I thought I owed it to you to look at my photos again before we got together tomorrow. After being sort of a jerk earlier."

"Aw, you admit you were a jerk. Isn't that nice?"

"I'm not joking. I'm being serious. Where are you?"

No, he wasn't joking. He was practically barking. "I'm on my way to the resort. I was bringing a peace offering to Aubrey."

"You might wanna wait on that."

"Why?" Besides, I was practically on the property. I wouldn't have to park in a garage this time, since I wasn't sneaking around.

"Because I found something interesting. I've been trying to get a hold of Sullivan but nobody seems to know where he is. Of all the times for him to decide to take a night off."

"Something worth calling him over? It must be bad."

"It might be. You should stay away from there."

"I'm practically already here. And there's no guarantee Aubrey or Kyle are even there. What's the big deal?"

"You want to know who kept feeding James Flynn champagne all night? It was Aubrey Klein."

I waited for more. When nothing came, I said, "Okay. And?"

"And that got me looking more closely at her. I studied every photo which included her. There was one which I took between the argument in the kitchen and going outside to find you crouched over the body where she's standing just inside the restaurant, in front of the windows."

"Okay?"

"There's sand on her feet. She was wearing those same strappy sandal shoes, like you wore."

"Not like I wore. Hers were maybe a thousand bucks more expensive," I snorted.

"Listen to me for a second, would you? There is most definitely sand on her feet in that picture. The way yours were after you were on the beach. I remember seeing it when we were at the police station."

He was looking at my feet?

I parked in front of the restaurant, on the opposite side of the pool and patio. There were lights on inside, but no movement. From this vantage point, I could almost put myself right back in the event.

"So, she had sand on her feet. Like I did, just as you said. Of course she did. It was sandy out there."

"But the body hadn't been discovered yet. I hadn't even gone outside looking for you. Do you see what I'm getting at?"

His voice filled the car. And my head. "She had already been on the beach," I whispered with a sick feeling. "Here I am, assuming Kyle's the killer and she's protecting him. But she was on the beach before James's body was discovered. Why would she have been out there?"

"And what are the odds that if she wasn't the killer, she happened to be on the beach and didn't see anything happening before coming inside? There's only that single path between the dunes, leading to and from the private beach. She had to cross through to come back inside. No way could she have avoided seeing something. If it wasn't her husband, wouldn't she say so?"

"Either she did it, or she saw who did but would rather Robbie go to prison," I breathed.

Something tapped against my passenger window, making me jump.

I turned to find a gun pointed at me through the window. And a redhead holding it.

"Turn off the car," she whispered. "Don't say a word."

"Emma?" Deke called out. "Where'd you go?"

Aubrey glared at me. "Hang up."

I hung up. A gun tended to remove the agony from decision making.

She opened the passenger door, looking inside the car while keeping the gun pointed at me. "Aww. Were these for me?" She picked up the plate of lemon bars which she most certainly did not deserve. "Come on. Inside. We have some talking to do."

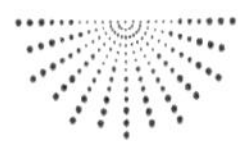

CHAPTER TWENTY-EIGHT

"Wow. Emma. Jeez, these are good." Aubrey polished off her third lemon bar, licking the fingers of the hand not holding the gun. "You could've been a pastry chef, sincerely. The crust is so rich, and there's just the right amount of sugar in them."

"Thanks?" It was hard to sound sincerely appreciative when somebody had a gun aimed at my head.

"So your friend the photographer is on to me, too, huh?" she asked. "I saw you pull up and recognized the car from earlier today, of course. I knew you were onto something. I just knew it. You couldn't leave well enough alone."

"I knew Robbie was innocent."

"Robbie's an idiot," she spat. "Getting hooked up with James, then thinking he can just pull out at the last minute? How did he think this place was going to survive without somebody like James Flynn running the resort? Why didn't he consider what it would mean to have somebody like James as an enemy? Because I assure you, he would've targeted my stupid husband after that. No doubt. This place would've tanked! I mean, everybody knows it takes years for a restaurant to turn a profit. He was willing to put our entire future on the line, and why? Because he's such a good guy and didn't wanna get wrapped up in something bad?" She gave an exaggerated pout before scoffing. "What a baby."

"He didn't tell you the details, did he? Only that he wanted out of their partnership." I clutched the chair on which I sat, afraid to make a move in case Aubrey got trigger happy.

Please, Joe, please, be somewhere. Be available. Get here soon. I only hoped Deke would keep calling him.

"My husband? Share details with me? Please. But I was smarter than he thought. Isn't that usually the way?"

"I guess so," I whispered.

"Please. Don't tell me those cops weren't urging you to mind your business. I talked to Joe Sullivan about you today. He apologized, told me you were an amateur detective and thought you knew better than the cops. But you knew enough to look at me as a suspect."

"Honestly? I thought it was your brother." Why bother lying now? She had a gun pointed at me.

"That's not fair," she chided. "Just because he got in trouble years ago. But that's just it. He needs this job. Now, he's running things. I don't know anything about the restaurant business, but he does. This is his big chance! I did this for him just as much as I did it for me. I had to look out for my own interests, since my husband wouldn't."

"I'm sorry to be the one to tell you this, but Robbie was trying to look out for you when he served James those papers. James was bankrupt, the books were sketchy at best, and Robbie was afraid he'd bankrupt the resort and leave you two holding the bag. You would end up being the ones to suffer for his poor decisions. That was why he wanted out of the partnership."

She blinked.

She blinked again.

"What?" she finally whispered, the gun trembling. "No. That's not true. That can't be true."

"I'm just saying, that's what he told me. That was why he didn't want to be partners with James. Not because James was a crook—which he was—but because Robbie knew he would do the same thing here. He already was! Yes, it was wrong that he didn't share his concerns with you. But how was he supposed to know what you'd do?"

She sat on a barstool, not ten feet from me, and burst out laughing. "You're kidding! Oh, jeez. That's what I get for assuming things. But it doesn't change the fact that my husband was an idiot for hooking up with him—against my advice, mind you—and that James would've done everything in his power to tank this restaurant to get back at him. So now, you could say I was protecting sweet Robbie, too. His beautiful dream." She snorted, looking around. "I mean, it came out nicely. Kyle will run it well. He'll make it a success."

"How did you do it without getting blood all over yourself?" I had to know. I just had to.

And darned if she didn't look proud of herself. "Well, for one thing, I put a couple of painkillers in James's champagne earlier in the night. He was feeling very, very good toward the end there, I'd bet. Those things don't mix, you know. You'll notice, or you might have, that Robbie only took a tiny sip of his drink."

"So he really was taking them heavily?"

"Ah, naw." She waved her free hand. "I only told you that so you'd think he was out of his mind. He was taking them for back pain after an old injury. Stress exacerbates the pain, but that's all. Only as much as he needed. Always playing it safe, my husband. Except when he didn't. When he made terrible choices."

"So you knew James would be a pushover because of the drugs and champagne."

"Literally," she snorted. "I pushed him over when I followed him outside. And he laughed, you know. He thought it was funny. He was so sleepy; he said that. No wonder, when he'd taken a couple of opiates along with alcohol. He was almost unconscious when I did it. One thrust of the knife and his eyes popped open, but it was too late. Bye-bye, scumbag. I grabbed the paperwork as an afterthought, but he hadn't even signed it so it didn't matter, really."

"Why weren't your prints on the knife?"

"Duh. I wore gloves from the kitchen. I'm not a doofus. Haven't you figured that out by now? I thought this through."

"Obviously. You fooled just about everybody."

"Just about." She waved the gun. "Come on. I think you're going for a swim."

"I didn't wear my suit."

"Ha, ha. Move." She was in front of me in an instant, hauling me to my feet.

"Jeez, you're strong," I observed.

"Yeah, once I added weight training to my workouts, that made all difference. It totally transformed my body." She yanked me toward the doors leading out to the patio and pool. "You're slim enough, but you could use some toning. Well, too late now."

"What are you gonna do? Shoot me and leave me on the beach? I mean, that's going to look suspicious, isn't it?"

"You're going to drown, dummy. I'm going to make you swim out as far as you can, and you're going to drown. Or else I'll shoot you. I'm an excellent shot."

It was dark, with only a sliver of a moon. But the lights from the sign atop the hotel tower provided enough illumination that she'd be able to see me in the water.

"It's still going to look suspicious, no matter how I died," I warned her. "My car is here."

"I'll get rid of it."

"Deke knows I was coming. So does my best friend. You won't get away with it."

"That's what you think. I've gotten away with it so far." She dragged me toward the dunes. I could hear the waves crashing further ahead, just like I'd heard them that fateful night.

This was another fateful night, wasn't it? I was going to drown. Even if I tried to swim away in the dark, she could follow me down the beach. I'd eventually tire, cramp up, go under. What a stupid way to die, but I was the one who'd be stupid enough to drive up with a plate of lemon bars and no backup.

"Come on." She led me to the water's edge, where it lapped up onto the sand. Cold, of course, since it was still April. I shivered as it swirled around my ankles.

"Keep moving," she ordered, nudging me with the gun in my back. "Go. Get out there. Don't bother trying to fight because you know I could take you down in a heartbeat. Too much time baking, not enough working out."

"I get it. You're super great at lifting weights. Jeez." That got me another poke in the back with the gun, and I took another step into the water. Then another one, shivering and on the verge of tears. Was this really happening? Was I going to die this way?

No. I wasn't. I couldn't go down without a fight. It was time to put those self-defense classes to use.

And the freezing cold water, too.

I turned, bending, and scooped up as much water and sand as I could hold before throwing it in Aubrey's face. She shrieked, her free hand going to her eyes.

I grabbed her wrist, pointing the gun upward. She squeezed the trigger and it went off, making me jump. At least it wasn't pointed at me.

We fell into the water, shrieking at the cold and at each other. I took a handful of her hair and thrust her head under the surface while trying as hard as I could to get the gun out of her hand. When the water receded, she sputtered and cursed and elbowed me in the ribs hard enough to knock the wind from my lungs.

She took advantage, throwing herself at me, knocking me onto my back. No matter what, I was not about to let go of her wrist.

Not even when another wave rolled in and covered my face. I kicked and squirmed, holding my breath, pushing on her arm so she couldn't lower it to fire at me. But I was getting weaker all the time.

"Aubrey Klein! This is the Paradise City Police Department!" A floodlight found us, blinding me with its brilliance. "Drop the weapon!"

I knew that voice, coming through the bullhorn. So somebody found Detective Joe, after all.

I also knew the man who dashed over moments later and pulled me to my feet.

"What are you doing here?" I asked, dazed and waterlogged and soaking wet and shaking as Deke wrapped me in his very warm arms.

"I was on my way down from my parents' house when I called. You hung up before I had the chance to tell you. I finally got a hold of Joe, and he told me to meet him here."

"Not a moment too soon," I observed, teeth chattering as he led me away from the water while two police officers took Aubrey into custody.

"Emma Harmon." Joe Sullivan looked me up and down before wrapping me in a blanket which I very deeply appreciated just then. "You're determined to be the death of me, aren't you?"

"Or the death of myself," I tried to joke. "It was nice hearing you yell at Aubrey and not me just now, though."

He chuckled, shaking his head. "I have to admit, nobody noticed the sand on Aubrey Klein's feet in that photo. Excellent detective work," he said to Deke, shaking his hand.

"And Robbie will be free now?" I asked, watching Aubrey as the police led her to a waiting car.

"As soon as the paperwork is processed," Joe promised. "I can't imagine it'll be easy for him, finding out his wife framed him for murder."

I hadn't thought of it in so many words until then, and

hearing it from Joe brought tears to my eyes. She'd framed my friend, somebody she was supposed to love.

I wished I'd had the chance to drown her.

"Come on," Joe beckoned. "Let's get you into the ambulance and to the hospital to get checked out."

"I'm fine."

"It's procedure when somebody is half-drowned," he assured me. "Imagine how much more work I'd have to do if you ended up getting sick because we were negligent."

"Ha, ha." I looked over my shoulder to where Deke stood, hands in his pockets. "I guess I won't be seeing you tomorrow," I called out, a little sad.

"You never know," he replied with a grin. I wondered what that meant.

Joe helped me into the ambulance, standing outside as I settled onto a gurney. "I called your father, and he's on his way," he explained.

"Oof. I can't wait to get an earful from him," I groaned, shivering in spite of the blanket.

"Yeah, well. Sometimes when people make us angry, it's because we care and don't wanna see them get hurt. Just… keep that in mind." He held my gaze for a long moment in which I forgot to breathe before taking a step back. "Be more careful from now on, Miss Harmon."

"Will do, Detective Sullivan." I watched him return to his team, where he barked orders like the tough cookie he was.

But even the toughest cookies could have a soft center. I suspected he was one of them.

CHAPTER TWENTY-NINE

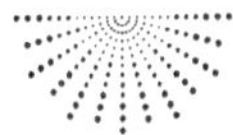

The last thing I expected to see on Sunday morning was a certain bleach blonde bimbo sliding an envelope under my windshield wiper as I stepped outside, ready to head to the café.

It was barely dawn, and she wore a black hoodie and yoga pants. Maybe she was on her way to an actual exercise class, or maybe she was out for a run.

Or maybe she wanted to be sneaky and leave a note while she thought I was sleeping. Silly girl. She didn't know the first thing about me.

Of course, I never learned her name while she was scrambling out of my bed, half-naked, so we both had things to learn.

"Excuse me?" I whispered, having sneaked up behind her. "What do you think you're doing?"

She jumped with a tiny squeal. Yes, I knew that squeal well. Exactly the sound she'd made when I discovered her and Landon. "I'm—I mean, I—that is—"

I had forgotten all about the note on my windshield after

almost drowning on Friday night. "So it was you, warning me to watch my back. Why? What did I do to you? What is even your name?"

"Naomi," she whispered, wide-eyed. So she was all talk and no action. Or, rather, all threats and no action. She hadn't even tried to run away.

"Okay, Naomi. Why the notes? What did I do to deserve this? It isn't enough that you were with my boyfriend in my bed? That I found you there? That my life took a nosedive for a hot minute?"

"What were you doing with him last weekend?" she challenged. "One of my friends saw you outside with him. Talking. He looked like he was apologizing."

"Huh? Oh! You mean when he came over and I wouldn't even let him upstairs because he doesn't deserve to step foot in what used to be our apartment? That was nothing. That was him trying to get on my good side. It didn't work."

"It didn't?"

"No. And that's it? You heard I was talking to your man, and it made you threaten me? That's a lot of suspicion when you've only been with him a few weeks. And don't tell me it went on for longer than that, because I don't wanna hear about it." Darned if she hadn't looked like she was going to do just that, too.

I almost wanted to hug the girl. She was so insecure. And wow, had I matured, since the last thing I wanted to do before that point was hug her. But face-to-face on the sidewalk in the early hours of the morning—when I'd had a near-death experience two days earlier—I had the chance to see things through different eyes.

"Naomi, I don't have any feelings for Landon anymore

except regret that I didn't see him for who he was before you did me a favor by showing me," I assured her with a smile. "If you don't trust him, that's on you. Believe me when I say he's all yours. Okay?"

She nodded, eyes still wide.

"Take the note with you," I ordered. "I don't wanna see what was inside the envelope. We'll pretend this never happened. Deal?"

"Deal," she whispered.

"Okay. I'm going to work. See you… hopefully never." But I knew better as I turned away to walk the familiar route to Mom's café. In a small town, there was exactly no chance of not running into each other. It was the risk I took.

And walking along the early morning streets reminded me of why I took such a risk. How could I not when there was so much history around me? Not just the town's history, which was rich enough, but my personal history. I was part of the tapestry, and it was part of me.

When I arrived at the café, as a few of the other business owners on Main Street began pulling up their metal grates to welcome the morning, I heard my mother giving orders in the kitchen.

"No, see, you need to beat the butter and sugar together long enough that it's fluffy and the color lightens. That means it's fully incorporated. And that you've whipped air into the mixture, which results in a lighter finished product."

I tiptoed to the swinging door, pushing it open just enough to peer inside. And what I saw was enough to make me clap a hand over my mouth to quiet my laughter.

Deke wore an apron over his usual button-down and

jeans, taking advice from my mother on how to properly cream butter and sugar. "Now, add the eggs one at a time, making sure to mix each one in thoroughly before adding the next."

He frowned in concentration, dropping one egg at a time into the bowl of the stand mixer. Mom nodded in approval while Darcy poured batter into muffin cups.

I couldn't resist. I had to know what was happening. "Excuse me?" I called out as I entered the kitchen. "Did I come to the wrong café?"

Mom practically tackled me. "I told you not to come in so early today! You need your rest, young lady!"

"Yes, but you know I can't sleep late. Somebody made sure of that as I was growing up." I patted her back, then turned my attention to Deke. "I didn't know you hired more help."

"Darcy, can you assist me with putting the chairs in place outside?" Mom asked, practically dragging my sister away from her work and leaving a puddle of muffin batter on the prep table.

"She's very subtle," Deke chuckled once we were alone.

"Yeah, subtlety is her strong suit," I agreed. "What are you doing here at this godawful hour of the morning, with powdered sugar all over you?" Indeed, he'd streaked it on his cheeks, his chin, his apron. I thought there might have been some in his hair, too.

"Since I couldn't get a hold of you yesterday, I wanted to be sure you couldn't avoid me forever. This seemed as likely a place to find you as any."

"That's a pretty big sacrifice to make, just so you could see me," I pointed out. "And if you had tried to call today, I probably would've answered. I had statements to make yesterday, good-intentioned neighbors to avoid…"

"I'm sure you were very busy," he grinned. "Still, I'm not big on patience."

He came around the table, standing in front of me. "I never did get to tell you how relieved I was that we made it to the beach when we did. Before anything happened."

"I'm glad, too," I smiled up at him. "I'm glad you were on your way when we talked. I'm glad you kept trying to get a hold of the police. I'm glad I had you on my side during this mess. I couldn't have done it without you."

"Even though I tried to convince you to move on and forget it?"

"You're forgiven," I sighed, reaching up to brush sugar from his chest. "You're also a mess. Maybe it's a good thing you didn't go into the candy business."

"And maybe it's a good thing you're not a comedienne." He took me by the waist, pulling me closer, while I cupped a hand around the back of his neck and pulled him down for a kiss made even sweeter thanks to the sugar on his lips.

His firm, skilled, delicious lips.

"Hmm," I grinned as I pulled away. "Not bad."

"You're only saying that because of the sugar," he winked. "I'll have to walk around with packets of it in my pockets the next time I'm back in town. But that won't be for a while, since Haute Cuisine is sending me to Seattle tomorrow, then Houston."

"Maybe we'll meet up somewhere in between," I suggested. "If not, you know where to find me. Right here."

"I'll make a point of it," he promised before another

quick kiss sealed the deal. This one was even sweeter, and it didn't have anything to do with sugar.

"Emma? You have a visitor!" Mom called out in an overly loud voice.

I groaned, though maybe it was for the best. Who knew what might've happened if we hadn't been interrupted?

"Robbie!" I managed to forget Deke's very nice mouth when I found Robbie Klein standing at the counter.

He held his arms out for a hug, kissing my cheek. "I had to come down and thank you. It's been a whirlwind, or I would've reached out yesterday."

"It was a whirlwind for me, too," I confessed. "I'm so glad you're free."

His smile wasn't completely bright, and I understood why. It had to be deeply conflicting, knowing it was his wife who'd put him in jail. But he looked better than he had just a few short days earlier, and that was a good start in my book.

Deke shook his hand. "Glad to see you free. What do you plan to do now? Or have you even given it any thought?"

"I have to admit, there's a lot in the air at the moment. Kyle swears he had no idea what Aubrey was doing, and she swears the same thing. He wants to stay on at the restaurant, and I don't see any reason why he shouldn't when none of this was his fault."

That was the Robbie I knew. That was what I couldn't get anybody else to understand before then. He didn't have a vengeful bone in his body.

"Otherwise, I have lawyers to help figure out the business end of things. I'd imagine I could sell to a management group and let them deal with that headache. I only want to run the restaurant. That's all that's ever interested me."

"The reviews that have come in so far are glowing," Mom assured him. "I've been following along."

"That's good to hear," he smiled.

"No big surprise. You have a hit on your hands, I'm sure of it." I gave him another hug. He deserved it. He deserved so much after what he'd been through.

"Promise you two will come in sometime soon for dinner," he said, looking to both me and Deke. "My treat."

Deke's brows lifted as he looked my way. "How's that sound to you?"

To me? Knowing my mother was listening and that news of this would spread like wildfire, there was still only one response that felt right. "Sounds like a date."

KEEP READING FOR AN EXCERPT FROM THE NEXT WINNIE Reed *Cape Hope Mysteries* selection.

EXCERPT: CORPSE IN A CRATE

CAPE HOPE MYSTERIES BOOK TWO

Emma's got a few days off and what better way to spend them than joining her best friend Raina on trip to a bed and breakfast Raina's former—maybe not so former?—crush is opening. Who knows, maybe she'll get a scoop for the blog. Wouldn't hurt to turn this into a working assignment.

Too bad everything falls to pieces when a body's discovered in a chest in the attic. Even worse, that Detective McHottie shows up in the middle of the investigation.

Can Emma figure out who is in the attic before the killer finds out she's looking into the matter?

He's got one question. How does she keep getting mixed up in these matters?

"Okay. It's time for you and me to have a little talk. I hate to do this, but you don't leave me any choice."

I looked her in the eye, forcing myself not to cave. This was too important to allow emotion to get in the way. If I didn't grow a spine and stick up for myself now, I'd be lost. Finished. There would be no hope of coming back from this.

"I should've done this before," I admitted, forcing myself to maintain eye contact. God, it was so hard to look into those cocoa-brown pools of light without whimpering like the weak-willed coward I was. I wanted to look away. I wanted to brush this latest transgression off as a mistake, or a misunderstanding.

She looked back at me, silent. Eyes wide, undoing me with their innocence. She couldn't possibly think she was in the right, could she? There was no excuse for her latest crime.

"Maybe it's my fault," I hedged, my voice cracking a little. I was no good, no good at all. There was no hope for me.

Glancing from the kitchen to the bedroom through the open door, I strengthened my resolve. All it took was a reminder of everything I'd lost.

"I should've made sure you knew how important they were to me," I allowed, "and I didn't. But that doesn't give you the right to destroy my property. I shouldn't have to tell you, should I? You should just respect what's mine because it's mine. You don't see me going around, destroying your belongings. If I'm bored, I do something constructive. I don't tear things to pieces."

I held up one of the two ruined sandals, waving it in front of her face. The other one was still on the floor at the foot of the bed, the leather straps chewed to pieces.

"This is no good, young lady. No good at all. I never even had the chance to wear them!" I looked at it, still as disappointed as I'd been when I first found the carnage. "I scored a huge clearance deal and was gonna wear them this weekend and pretend I paid full price, but now that's out the window."

Lola blinked up at me, her little puppy head tilting to the side in that way that absolutely killed me. I mean, it reduced me to a puddle. She owned me, and she knew it.

"I know you don't know what you did, but you're still a bad girl. Bad girl." I waved the sandal in her face, hoping to stir memories of her crime. To her credit, she ducked her head a little.

"Darn right, you're sorry and you'll never do it again." Did I sound stern enough? I hoped so. "And you'd better not act up while you're with Grandmom this weekend. It's one thing to ruin my brand-new Steve Maddens, but another thing to ruin anything of hers. She'll start in on the whole *If this were an actual grandchild and not a ten-pound dog, we wouldn't be having these issues* thing, and my head might explode."

I picked her up, nuzzling the top of her cotton fluff head. "And then who would give you treats, huh?"

At the mention of the t-word, Lola scrambled out of my grasp and turned rapid circles on the floor, her ears flopping, her mouth open in what I tried to tell myself was a smile.

Truly, the dog owned me. All I could do at that sort of reaction was shrug, reach into the bag and toss a treat her way. Who was I to deny that sort of joy? I wasn't a monster.

While she feasted—and, as such, received the message that her bad behavior was something worth being rewarded for, God I was a dope for that dog—I went back to my room and kicked the ruin sandal aside in favor of checking my bags. It was only a weekend away with Raina, but anything was possible while traveling with her. She had a way of throwing a wrench into the works.

But in a nice way. In a *I found the most amazing four-star restaurant where lots of rich people like me go to eat and drink champagne and chuckle over how wonderful we are* sort of way.

As such, I'd packed a Little Black Dress and pumps for the occasion, with a small purse to match. Otherwise, my two carry-on size suitcases were full of jeans, t-shirts, sundresses and jammies. I'd even packed a bathing suit and coverup in case Raina had scored a hotel with a nice pool.

Which I assumed she had, because this was Raina. The girl traveled in style, even if she was only staying near an old friend's farmhouse in Maryland.

"Come on," I called out to my outlaw puppy, whose

mother I'd been for all of a month. "Time to go visit with Granny, so she can spoil you with goodies she's not supposed to give you and then call me and complain when you go on a sugar-fueled reign of terror."

I wished I was making that part up, but I wasn't.

I strapped Lola into her little harness—everything was so little, the cuteness killed me—and slung the bag full of toys, treats and puppy food over one shoulder before walking her down the stairs and out onto the sidewalk. Mr. Angelo was busy tossing dough behind the window of his pizza shop, but he always took time to wave to the dog and me as we passed.

I had the feeling he liked Lola better than he liked me, but that was okay. I liked her better than some people, too.

Besides, it wasn't like Lola could shove cash his way whenever she'd had a trying day or a long week. She wasn't the one who'd been consuming his pizzas for years and probably putting his kids through college with the profits.

It was a glorious May morning, only two weeks shy of Memorial Day. Already there was a great deal more activity around Cape Hope which was poised to explode at the start of the summer season. I took in the fresh awnings, smartly-painted trim along the storefronts, pretty flowers in brand-new planters flanking entrances. Everybody put their best foot forward at this time of year, looking forward to months of healthy profits.

Including my mother, though business never exactly slowed down. Sweet Nothings was the meeting place for those in Cape Hope who called it home all year long, just as it had been since I was barely out of the womb.

As such, everybody who walked through the door felt like they had a vested interest in my life. Lucky me.

"There's Lola!" Breanna Schultz stood at the counter in Mom's café when I strode through the door with my dog, waiting for a cup of green tea or whatever yoga enthusiasts drank after a class. I wouldn't have known since I stopped practicing maybe three minutes after I started.

"And me," I added with a smirk. "I feel like my only purpose in life now is to take my Maltese from place to place so people can adore her."

"You do such a good job of it." Breanna winked my way before crouching in front of Lola, scratching her behind the ears. And what did my beloved puppy do in response? She rolled over onto her back, belly exposed, her brown eyes silently beseeching.

"She'll do anything for a belly scratch," I scowled indulgently.

Breanna did as she was told, since after all, we were merely there for the dog's enjoyment, before standing with a mile-wide smile. "When am I gonna see you at the studio again?" she asked, all glowy and dewy after exercising her body in a way I rarely did.

Nothing like that deer-in-headlights feeling. "Uh, soon. I think."

She laughed. "You know I'm only teasing. I love watching you squirm."

"Thanks."

My mother turned to face us, holding a cup filled with ice and fresh tea, just like I'd guessed. "She's too busy jet-setting all over the place for her job," she practically crowed.

"I wouldn't call it that," I blushed. "I was only in Fort Lauderdale last week."

"And Chicago the week before that," she prompted. "Writing about restaurants, getting paid to travel and eat well. Can you imagine how much fun that would be?"

Sometimes she laid it on a little too thick. "Breanna knows what I do, Mom. Everybody does. You make a point of telling them."

Breanna laughed. "It's nice, seeing a mom being so proud of her daughter. At least she doesn't get on your case about only owning a yoga studio and not doing something more substantial with your life."

"Now, if only I could have a grandchild and not a grand-doggie, my life would be complete," Mom sighed in her usual dramatic fashion before turning her attention to a new customer I didn't recognize. A tourist, in other words.

"My mother," I whispered, waving a hand her way with a flourish.

Breanna giggled. "Where are you headed this weekend? Another assignment?"

"Not this time. My friend Raina is bringing me along to visit an old family friend. He's renovating a farmhouse that's been in the family for centuries, turning it into a bed and breakfast down in Maryland. I was thinking of pitching the place as a potential assignment later, once it's open."

"Ooh, that sounds lovely. I haven't had a vacation in so long. I need a B&B weekend."

"You'll have to come with me when it opens," I offered. She was a nice person, and she'd been probably the only saving grace at the disastrous book club meeting at Mom's during the Riviera Resort Murder Case, as the newspapers had taken to calling it in the weeks afterward.

That, and all the sangria my sister kept pouring for me while I was grilled on the details of the case by half the women in town.

Meanwhile, Mom was deep in conversation with a tourist who could not have cared less about my personal life. "There was a very handsome photographer in her life for roughly five minutes, but she managed to frighten him away."

I wanted to die, which seeing as how I'd been in the café for maybe three minutes was par for the course. "Mom. Please. I didn't scare anybody away," I hissed, ushering Lola into the kitchen and away from the sympathetic and bewildered gaze of a middle-aged man who just wanted a cup of coffee.

"Then why hasn't he called in weeks?" she asked, shrugging. The very picture of motherly innocence, only concerned for her daughter's happiness—despite the fact that she'd just finished complaining about having no grandchildren.

"He has a life. Work. So do I." The fact was, I had no idea why Deke Bellingham had dropped off the face of the earth, but I hardly felt like discussing it either with my mother or with a dozen patrons listening in on every word.

Maybe I'd dodged a bullet. He could be hopelessly annoying and remote and sarcastic, and I didn't need that in my life. So what if he could wear a pair of jeans better than any man I'd ever known? And so what if he'd called the police and arrived at the Riviera in time to save me from being murdered by Aubrey Klein?

For that matter, so what if I'd consumed my weight in Mr. Angelo's pizza and my mother's blueberry muffins in the weeks since Deke decided he didn't have time to return a phone call?

Life went on, and I was about to embark on a weekend getaway with my best friend. Things could be worse.

Even so…

I dropped to a crouch in front of Lola, who waited patiently for me to set up her doggie bed in one corner of the kitchen. "Be on your best behavior this weekend, young lady," I whispered, kissing her fluffy head. "If she starts squawking at me about you not being an acceptable replacement for a grandbaby, I don't know what I'll do."

I hope you enjoyed *Stiff in the Sand*!
For more Winnie Reed books click here!

Sign up for the newsletter to be notified of new releases.

Click on link for
Newsletter